HYPOTHERMIA

Originally published as *Hipotermia* by Anagrama,
Barcelona and Mexico City, 2005.

Copyright © 2005 by Álvaro Enrigue
Translation © 2013 by Brendan Riley

First edition, 2013

Enrigue, Alvaro, 1969-
[Hipotermia. English]
Hypothermia / Alvaro Enrigue ; Translated from the
original Spanish to English by Brendan P. Riley. -- First
Edition.
pages cm
"Originally published as Hipotermia by Anagrama,
Barcelona and Mexico City, 2005."
ISBN 978-1-56478-873-3 (pbk. : alk. paper)
I. Title.
PQ6705.N63H4713 2013
863'.64--dc23
2013001673

Partially funded by a grant from the Illinois Arts Council,
a state agency

www.dalkeyarchive.com

Cover: design and composition by Mikhail Iliatov

HYPOTHERMIA

ÁLVARO ENRIGUE

TRANSLATED BY BRENDAN RILEY

DALKEY ARCHIVE PRESS
CHAMPAIGN / LONDON / DUBLIN

CONTENTS

I'm a really first-rate writer. Nobody knows it, but it's true—that's what I said to my son yesterday. It wasn't the first time; I usually say it when I've had too much to drink. What you are, he responded, looking me straight in the eye, is a run-of-the-mill pen pusher at a second-rate newspaper. He'd also had too much to drink. I'm a writer, I repeated. Maybe I'm a lousy one, but I'm still a writer. I'd never used that one before. But his retort left me in the shade. With cocksure cruelty, he smiled—a smile I've lived with since he was a boy—and said: Yeah, right. You ever gonna get a book published? Real writers publish books.

I left the table and went and locked myself in the bathroom where I sat down on the toilet to have a smoke. I could hear Estela scolding my son. She was reminding him—*Allow me to remind you*, she said, which meant that they'd already argued about it before—that I'd stopped working on my own writing full time the minute she told me she was pregnant. He wanted you to have the same privileges your grandfather gave him, my wife continued. Your father never could've paid for all the things you've had just by writing essays. Not to mention books. Well, they were so good nobody wanted to publish them.

Estela's version of things isn't entirely accurate, but by now it's become a set piece in our family mythology. We all like to believe that's the way things went. But, first off, I've always had a steady job. How else could I support the intensely literary life we've led all these years? It's impossible to even dress like a writer, for example, on what you earn from writing. We never lived off my writing. At the most the stuff I published provided us with drinking money—and they were pretty cheap drinks at that. And then, it was only *one* of my books that nobody wanted to publish, for the simple reason that it was the only one I ever finished. But at that moment, locked in the bathroom, smoking, I was in no mood to quibble over little things like the truth.

I finally came out when I was sure that Sebastián had left the apartment. Estela was washing the dishes. Without saying a word, I poured myself another glass of anís then came and sat down at my desk here in the den and lit another cigarette. The unspoken rules of the house state that I can smoke all I like when I'm sitting here. However much it stinks up the house, it's tolerated because it would be worse if I closed the door behind me. Also, here I can drink alone without arousing suspicion. I take refuge in the myth that alcohol and writing go hand in hand.

Thirty or thirty-five years ago, anyone would've been surprised if you'd told them that I would end up dedicating myself to something other than literature. Our whole circle of friends was quite familiar with my vocation, and given the speed with which I had risen in literary circles, most of them thought that I had a good chance of achieving some success. A few, Estela chief among them, were sure that I'd become really famous. Back then, she was a naïve, dazzling young thing, and I had plenty of charisma—I still do, in fact, but I've got no interest in dusting it off. One day at dinner with some quasi-distinguished guests—nobody really special—a very drunken acquaintance described Estela and me as *a Renaissance couple*. And to a certain extent we were: we frequented vintage booksellers, attended concerts and exhibitions, and took long trips around the country. We could talk cinema and dance gracefully. We didn't have much money—very little, in fact—but we never wanted for very much. Our families helped us out, as much as they could, but we never abused their generosity.

Estela still believes, or maybe she's just in the habit of believing, or perhaps she's only allowing me to believe that she believes, that I will one day manage to write a publishable book. I also believed it, at least until yesterday when I saw that cruel, familiar smile. It's true that my son has given me the best moments in my life, even if getting at them has sometimes been like pulling teeth. Perhaps the only thing left for him to give me was this entirely unappreciated, yet totally decisive, liberation.

When Estela finished washing the dishes she came to the den to say goodnight. She had something to tell me but kept it to herself: seeing me in front of the computer makes her curiously respectful, as if I were really capable of writing something worthwhile.

Naturally, this wasn't the case: I was working on the article that I turned in today for the *Living* section. My editor loved it. With his repulsive, petulant, faggoty pronunciation, he once again recommended that I quit Personnel and dedicate myself to real writing. It's never too late, he told me. I told him that I'd wait until retirement to start writing full time. I said this out of habit, without even thinking about it. He offered to help me whenever I took the plunge: he had friends with inside connections. I kept my scoffing to myself; what could his friends offer a man like myself? As I was leaving his office, my right hand touched the gold fountain pen in my shirt pocket, a gift from my sister when I finished my B.A. We call it *la pluma de Dumbo*, which is to say—because *pluma* is *plume* is *feather* is *quill* is *pen*— *Dumbo's feather*, because until today it's always been my good-luck charm: I've used it to write the first page of every one of my unfinished novels. As I walked along the hallway I tapped the pen against my palm a few times, thinking ahead to the afternoon and the tequila I was going to have for an aperitif. Sebastián would order a vodka tonic. It's always the same: I drink Herradura and he drinks Absolut. I pick the wine for dinner. For a nightcap, he has Carlos I brandy and I have dry Chinchón anís on the rocks.

After I finished typing the article that the idiot from *Living* loved so much, I went to bed. Estela was still awake. She must have assumed I was depressed about what Sebastián had said and was feeling the need for some well-deserved consolation: the truth was that neither wife nor son knew that after mulling over Sebastián's comments, I couldn't help but agree with him. She hugged me tightly and we ended up making love like a couple of elephants; we're too old and out of shape to do it any other way. We finished, and as she lay there panting she told me that Sebastián had asked me to forgive him for being rude. He wanted to take me out to eat at Los Alamos, a place I really like.

He's a good-hearted kid. And even if he isn't, at least he keeps his word. He called me at eleven-thirty, when I had just come back from turning in my article. After we said hello, he asked me how I was doing. Between sighs I said that I was fine. Well, it doesn't sound like it, he told me. Without softening the rueful tone in my voice I mentioned that I was having problems at work. Anything serious? he asked. Just the usual stuff. He suggested that we have lunch together so that I could tell him about it. I said that I'd love to but I couldn't because on days when I'm in a bad mood I prefer to eat alone at my desk. He begged me to go to Los Alamos with him to see if that would cheer me up. We agreed to meet at three-thirty.

I had a bit of work to finish but no real desire to do it, so I locked the door, drew the blinds, and settled into an armchair to wait for lunch, planning my new life. At three o'clock on the dot I got up, slapped on some cologne, and headed out. We arrived at the restaurant within a few minutes of each other. He had obviously been hard at work until the very last minute, and he showed up looking nervous: he only remembered to take off his jacket when he was already sitting down.

Unlike me, Sebastián is the kind of person who loves and respects his job. Thanks to which we have ammunition for another of our endless arguments. He says that his profession demands a great deal of responsibility—I can forget to sign a check and it's no big deal: a slight delay for some anonymous payee; whereas if he miscalculates the weight of this or that material going into some structure, his oversight could cost countless lives. Whenever he mentions it, I remind him that I was opposed to his studying engineering. A career like that, I always told him, will bring you nothing but problems and frustrations. But in spite of the never-ending sarcasm that I heap on him, he often seems proud of having succeeded in his profession. Once he even told me that if I'd let him watch television like other kids, he would've studied humanities; he's sure that the torturous afternoons I spent expounding on the virtues of the *Young People's Treasure Chest Encyclopedia* turned him away from culture for good. Today I tell myself that he might actually have a point, but it's far too late for regrets.

While I watched him struggling to get his jacket off without standing back up, it occurred to me that I might be able to make him suffer just a little bit more if I pretended to be depressed. Then again, that might suck all the life out of the act I was about to perform. I put on a radiant expression. Sebastián said that I seemed to be in a much better mood than when we'd spoken on the phone. I told him that things had gotten better at the office, and then I signaled the waiter.

Your usual? he asked. Yes, I answered with satisfaction, then said nothing. After a rather uncomfortable silence Sebastián said, I see you've got Dumbo's feather. Are you starting a new novel? Such a blatantly conciliatory reference to my literary problem meant that he really was worried about his idiotic comments the night before. No, I replied, and lapsed back into silence, enjoying his nervousness.

There was nothing more to say until the waiter returned with our drinks. Sebastián's vodka was served on the rocks along with a small bottle of tonic. I threw back my tequila in a single gulp. Another, sir? the waiter asked. The same. Sebastián was alarmed: he'd never seen me drink like that. He mustered his courage, took the bull by the horns, and said: I went too far last night. Instantly I raised my hand, cutting him off: Before you say another word, just pour your tonic. To his credit, he obeyed me, which—it's worth saying—he's almost always done, except when it came to engineering. While he poured the tonic water into his vodka I took Dumbo's feather out of my shirt pocket and ceremoniously unscrewed the cap right under his nose. If that startles you, I said to him, I don't even want to imagine what you'll think about this. And for my next act I sank the pen right into his glass. The ink billowed out, rising toward the ice cubes like a plume of smoke from a cigarette. He looked scandalized, I'm not sure whether this was on account of my strange behavior or because I was spoiling his vodka. Then I stirred his drink with my personal swizzle stick, saying: Here, this is a gift. Dumbo's feather, especially for you. I'm only a run-of-the mill pen pusher at a second-rate paper but I'm doing just fine. Then I got up and walked straight out of the restaurant, right past the astonished face of the waiter who was just coming back with my second tequila.

Estela didn't bring it up during dinner, so I have to

assume Sebastián is so confused he hasn't even called her. Maybe he actually thinks his rude remarks last night killed off what remained of my sanity. He might be right. Here I am sitting in front of the computer with my anís and my cigarette, and the words are flowing like never before. Perhaps tomorrow after dinner I'll feel like a smoke, and not in the bathroom. I'll plant myself here, and to justify my drinking I'll begin some story; nothing literary, just a sad little story, to be followed by others like it. They'll be stories about people who aren't working through difficult questions or pathetic feelings; minor characters—people who've never visited Paris, people nobody cares about. Gringos, for example. Normal, everyday gringos like the tourists you see on the street in their Bermuda shorts. Or maybe not. Maybe I'll donate all the books that I've taken such pains to collect. I'll give away my computer and sell my writing desk. Then I'll buy myself a soft, overstuffed couch and a big screen TV, and I will make this den my masterpiece.

Scenes from Family Life

In the ever-dreadful and overvalued popular imagination, a commercially successful writer is something that one comes to be, not something that one once was. For a surprising number of months, I was the rather relieved, but secret, author of a bestseller. Perhaps that's hard to believe, but I swear it's true.

My stunningly casual and entirely wasted trip through the bestseller list happened even before the beginning of my laborious and, frankly, long-suffering career as a writer. I was about twenty-five or twenty-six, living a disheveled sort of life that got rolling each day around noon—at the earliest. I had a certain reputation as a hard-line literary critic, but little else. It was a disaster in the making, thanks to these and a few other factors. For one, I'd recently lost a good job at a private university press: they'd discovered that I was using office hours to translate self-help books—for which I was miserably paid. For another, my wife, Cathy, made the unilateral decision that the time had arrived for making babies, so she stopped teaching classes at an English-language academy the better to cook one up. And then, the last straw, I'd run up an enormous debt on the three different credit cards which were burning a hole right through my wallet.

During one of those elegant lunches that nobody in our austere literary republic can really afford, I blamed the editor of the self-help books whose translations had cost me my job with its medical insurance and supermarket vouchers. I was already drunk enough that, with all the ingratitude appropriate to my condition, I made a number of unflattering remarks about the guy's business. Responding with an unexpected professional pride—which itself probably only flourished when watered with tequila—he said that if I'd ever paid any real attention to the books he published, my own life might not be so depressing and miserable. I put up with his gibe mainly because I agreed with him about the depression and misery, but I told him that his books were so terrible I'd never even read the ones I'd translated. Sitting there, staring at me with the superior look of one who's had slightly more to drink than his companion, the editor puffed out his cheeks, pressed his lips together, and said that that was impossible: one necessarily reads what one is writing as you go along. Then, *mea culpa*, instead of pissing myself laughing, I decided to brag. I told him that I could write one of his books from beginning to end by working just one hour a day and without rereading a single fucking word. He replied that he'd be sending me a contract the next day to see what I was really made of. The company courier woke me up at eleven o'clock the next morning to sign for it.

Unlike contracts for completed literary works, the ones for self-help books include a sort of instruction sheet about how to write them: being strictly commercial products, they follow tight guidelines that come spelled out in precise legal terms: the book must have a certain number of chapters and each chapter must be composed of X number of pages made up of paragraphs of no more (or less) than, for example, five sentences, each with a maximum of three clauses. The book's theme and even the title come pre-specified—the result of a marketing survey—and you've got to promise, or risk forfeiting your advance, to deliver the book by a certain date, which in my case was four weeks from the day of signing. The book's title, as assigned me by the publisher, was: *Discipline: White Magic for the Successful Man.*

After carefully reading the contract I thought of asking for six months to deliver the book. My wife, however—reading over my shoulder in a most irritating way—pointed out that it would perhaps be worth my while to make more of an effort: she was already seven months pregnant and my credit cards couldn't even bear the brunt of her hospital registration fee. I went ahead and signed.

At first I tried to maintain the schedule I'd been enjoying, unearned—playing the literary celebrity: rise at noon, eat lunch with some minor luminary with whom I would then, preferably, spend the afternoon drinking, then head home—if there wasn't some book launch or publishing house cocktail party—eat dinner, drink several cups of coffee, and spend half the night writing.

I quickly realized that if I kept working that way I would never finish the damn thing. The pressure of the coming birth was considerable, but what really spurred me on was my own twisted sense of dignity—I couldn't bear the thought of losing my drunken boast. And then, my lifestyle didn't even give me the time I needed to be able to read the books and write the reviews and articles thanks to which we barely paid for the rent on our garret and our necessarily vegetarian diet. So I began to get up at the same time that Cathy left for her walk in Venados Park, to write more or less mechanically for the first two or three hours of the morning. Then I would make corrections nonstop until lunchtime. In the afternoon I worked on my old hard-line articles then went to bed at a reasonable hour so I could be up and writing the goddamn self-help book at the break of dawn the next day.

I don't have a very happy memory of those rather melancholy weeks, but the robotic routine of concentrated work made me feel, for the first time, like a responsible adult member of the self-respecting middle class for whose defense and perpetuation—like it or not—I was raised and educated.

I finished the book on time and submitted it, resplendent in victory, honor untarnished, for publication under a pseudonym. It was disgraceful. We spent my advance on the fee for the birth and a two-month supply of diapers, then used the rest to pay off one of my credit cards.

It didn't take long before money was tight again. You're going to have to nurse him until he's fifteen, I told my wife, but then we received the first sign of a positive change in my professional life: the public relations woman at my publisher began to call every day asking me if I would give interviews. It sounded like fun so I did a few over the telephone, but to avoid tarnishing my proud career as a readerless critic I never consented to do them for radio, or television, or for anybody, really, who might want to broadcast any evidence of my real identity. On the phone I made sure to project a zealous belief in all the ridiculous bullshit my book contained.

I had just asked to borrow some money from my father—my credit cards were now more maxed out than ever—when I received the first check, the first amazing royalty check from sales of the book. I'll just say this: we went to Italy for six months so we could take care of the baby in comfort and ease. When we returned there were two more checks waiting: we bought a car and there was so much money left over that when the next one arrived we bought the whole apartment that contained the little au pair suite where we had been living. From then on our capital gains grew thinner, but we didn't notice it so much because I was already earning more, working in the mornings translating better-paying books for a more respectable press.

I'm not going to say that we weren't disappointed the first quarter when a royalty check didn't show up, but by then it wasn't such a big deal. Cathy had taken on some private students and I was completely focused on spending the afternoons working on what turned out to be my first novel, which sold a grand total of four hundred and twenty-three magnificent copies.

GULA, OR: THE INVOCATION

One fine day, with no particular destination in mind, we found ourselves brainstorming ideas about how to escape from Mexico City. For my part, at least, I couldn't stand the place anymore. The current government as well as the opposition party; my coworkers; my neighbors and their endlessly rude, spoiled children; having to wait in line at the bank to file my quarterly tax returns: it had all become insufferable. As we had a little money saved up, we figured we could move—without too much hardship—to some new and exciting foreign city. After shuffling through a bunch of possibilities, our deliberations ended with our settling on two possible locations: one, glamorous and risky, where we could continue living out our intensely bohemian life; the other, more secure, where I could work as a university professor. It was July; we set our departure for January and decided to let fate choose our destination.

Moving abroad is a lot more work than it seems: we ended up spending nine months getting everything in order. Then, on a day like any other, I ran into an old astrologer friend—as serious and professional a fellow as his profession allows—in the produce aisle at the supermarket. Being well-versed in the Ancient Greek tragedies, I've always been reluctant to visit him for advice. He did draw up my star chart once, but I was altogether too anxious to sit down and read the results.

That day in the store he told me that he'd been thinking about me and that perhaps it was time for us to have a proper consultation. So I went, casting my lot with ancient superstitions—who knew, perhaps it would give our life a direction, pointing out which city would be luckiest for us.

On my one and only visit to his study, I quickly learned the cold, hard truth about the stars: nothing so banal as points on a map ever show up in your horoscope. What I was shown instead was a descent into hell, with death at either end. First, a terrible one in February. Someone in your family, he said, your mother, your son, Cathy, one of your brothers or sisters. Then another one, later on, between April and August, which, if I didn't take precautions, would be my own.

There was even more bad news to come, albeit of a less fatal variety. You're going to lose your job in December, he told me, by way of example. That's because I'm giving notice, I answered. I'm moving away in January. No, he insisted, they're going to fire you and you'll leave town after April. If you stay alive, that is. My favorite cat also showed up in my friend's visions, an ill-tempered black Persian. There's an animal here, he told me, who seems to be the protector of your house. That's Gula, I told him. She'd give her life, he added, to save you or any of your family.

Now that we'd finished I asked him if there were any sort of talisman he could recommend that might protect me. We were staring out his office window at a dingy, trash-strewn street. You're a writer, aren't you? he asked. More or less, I told him. So write it all out. Sometimes that can work like a lightning rod.

Remembering, like storytelling, means creating order where none existed. The truth is that my session with the astrologer was much more confusing than the above, and his statements far less clear. But, regardless, I left his office feeling disturbed by something but uncertain of what this might be—sort of like the way you feel after drinking too much coffee. Back home I gave my wife a deliberately abbreviated version of my session, minus all the disgraceful catastrophes that were looming ahead. And because it's better to prevent than lament, I began to write, almost furtively, a story about a cat that sacrifices itself for a man and his children.

December arrived and they fired me from the company where I'd worked for years. You said that you were leaving in January anyway, so we made our own plans, my boss told me, trying to make it sound like it was nothing personal. As if it could ever not be personal. Around the beginning of February, during the same weeks I was fleshing out my story about the cat's death, the police rang my doorbell in the middle of the night. They had my brother—one of nine siblings—locked up in the back of their patrol car with a cracked sternum and fractured ribs. They brought him like that, and at such an unlikely hour, because in a near-fatal accident he'd flattened a lamppost, which constituted a civil offense.

By that time we had already closed out our bank accounts, so I ran upstairs for a roll of cash. We settled on a price and I paid up. I also tipped generously so that they would dispose of my brother's horrifyingly wrecked car, and so that the officers would forget our names and addresses forever. I took my brother to the hospital.

When I returned home many hours later, Cathy asked me if this had been the trouble I'd been expecting. What trouble? I asked her. What the astrologer predicted for you. Astrologers don't *predict* anything, I told her. My brother's going to be fine, don't worry. I left the story about the cat unfinished and went back to work on the book that was due to be published before we moved.

At last, my wife and I finished almost everything that we had begun in Mexico City, and in the middle of May, in one momentous effort, we left the country with our little boy, our cat, and our piano. Since my second book had already gone on sale and our university jobs in the hardly glamorous city to which we'd moved didn't begin until after August, I decided to get back to my story about the man and the cat before classes started. As much as I disliked the idea of having to finish the poor beast off, I felt an overwhelming sense of metaphysical responsibility demanding I write out its demise. You always have to finish what you start, especially if the warring stars above augur your misfortune.

At the beginning of August we moved to our new, permanent address. There, Gula and I and our little boy began to enjoy spending time in the garden, a real novelty for us. At night I worked on the story about the cat and the man.

Gula had always been insufferably independent, but she'd never had any direct experience of the outdoors. Now she spent entire days hunting mice and exploring trees: she'd never even seen one before. Meanwhile, I finally killed the cat in the story I was writing.

When one's imagination runs dry, superstition is its last refuge, but superstition—once invoked—goes right on menacing us even when we have no need of it anymore, even when we deny its reality: no one really believes that such invocations have any effect on the world; we're rational people after all, but we still knock on wood! One morning we noticed that Gula hadn't come home to sleep in our bed for a few nights. I went down to the basement and found her—the epitome of feline vanity—stretched out, feverish and dusty, under an air-conditioning duct. We took her to the vet. It turned out that she'd eaten a poisonous root that had destroyed her liver—she had only a few hours left to live. We carried her back home. There we made her a comfortable bed of towels and old scraps of flannel, and we let her die in peace.

9:00 A.M. Before my son was born I used to spend whole days at the beach, as though I were already retired. Not that I ever went out to dance clubs or sipped cocktails from coconut shells, nor was I ever one of those adrenaline junkies who risk their necks parasailing. Instead I'd sit, just planted in the sand, reading a book. It runs in my family. When we were kids, my parents frequently took us to spend weekends at the beach. These were only weekend trips, so we made sure to enjoy every moment to the fullest extent. We'd arrive late on Friday evening. Then, on Saturday morning, we'd eat breakfast in shifts so that we could secure a palapa facing the sea, right at the edge of the surf, where we would all settle in for the day: my parents imperiously enthroned in the shade, and the nine of us children—brazenly lazy, almost obscenely identical—stretched out reading in a row of beach chairs like a flank of cavalry.

Ever since my son was born, however, a day on vacation is more like a feverish trance: from six A.M. to eight each morning we're in the swimming pool; then it's time for breakfast and off to the beach. There we tumble in the waves, dig holes, build sandcastles, make seaweed wigs, and poke around for crabs to torture. I end up with sand encrusted on parts of my body I didn't even know existed. Around noon we retreat to the house's air-conditioned embrace. We eat lunch, then I put my son down for his nap. In the afternoon, while Cathy is looking after him, I settle down—as in days gone by—to read a paperback edition of *The Odyssey*. Perhaps being a father now helps me to see that all the tension in Homer's epic comes from the friction between the hyperkinetic Odysseus and the placidly dim-witted

Telemachus, a good-for-nothing son who neither defends his mother from the pretenders who accost her, nor sets sail in search of his father.

Today is different. We're staying at an enormous house on the Outer Banks of North Carolina, a strip of sandbars and islands which begins at Cape Henry, just a few miles from Norfolk, and stretches south more than three hundred miles, beyond Cape Fear and Wilmington—a haven for pirates, once upon a time. We—my wife, our little boy, a pair of grandmothers, two dogs, and a cat—opened up the house last Sunday and we'll close it next week. It's now Wednesday, maybe Thursday. The day before yesterday the rest of my wife's family arrived. Because they live far inland, up in the hills, they hate—possibly without realizing it—the sea and everything to do with it. One day at the beach was enough to convince them that there's no sport in tormenting crabs—they walk backward, after all—and spur them to organize a few outings in the car, with seat belts properly buckled and the air-conditioning high enough to blow-dry their hair. Through gritted teeth, my wife angrily gave in to her family obligations—the inexorable summons of her bloodline—so she and our son are heading out with them for the day. I'm staying here to get some work done.

As I helped to pack the Diet Cokes and the party-size bags of Tostitos as big as TV sets, I was seized by the dizzying prospect of spending an entire day of perhaps immoral peace and quiet: in the gringo universe, where having children is more a self-indulgent whim than a real decision, one quickly learns that if your kids aren't driving you crazy, it's because they're driving someone else crazy, somebody without kids of their own.

10:30 A.M. From the spacious third-floor balcony you can

see the ocean. Between our place and the beach is another row of houses similar to this one. People around here christen their homes as they do their yachts. Each one has its own sign emblazoned with some quasi-nautical name: *Circe*, *Ogygia*, *Poseidon*. The breeze is not especially refreshing and I feel sorry for my relatives driving around out there. By now they must have reached the town of Kitty Hawk where, in 1903, the Wright Brothers defied gravity with their tiny, pathetic first flight, which lasted all of twelve seconds. Since then we've never stopped perpetuating that defiance: we fly to Tokyo, we stay up all night drinking Diet Coke, we make babies for the hell of it.

The ocean is tempting but the books I'm reading are checked out from the university library, and it looks bad if you return them all greasy, stained with Coppertone. This house—somebody else's—feels very strange, its quiet emptiness closing in around me. I never really thought I could miss my oversized brothers-in-law.

11:00 A.M. The conquest of the Canary Islands was a strange thing, really more of a sudden interruption in the midst of timeless tranquility. In one of her books, the Cuban Professor Eyda Merediz—like myself, an émigré to Washington, D.C.—writes that Spain's incorporation of the Fortunate Isles into its Empire provided a model for subsequent Spanish incursions into the Americas: Columbus's bizarre descriptions of his first landing in the West Indies result from his perceiving Atlantic America through the nascent mythology of the Canary possessions. This probably also accounts for the perverse insistence on seeing our own tormented continent as an Edenic territory: what those Spanish captains found on the Canaries was nothing like the complex, militarized civilizations that Cortés or Pizarro fought to conquer, but a separate universe, infinitely isolated in its megalithic serenity. The German anthropologist Hans Biedermann has shown that, before being assimilated into Spanish culture, the Guanches were the last bastion of the European Stone Age: despite a reliance on draft animals they neither used wheels nor forged metals.

In settling personal feuds, the Guanches practiced a custom that, as recorded by various historians, seems to me particularly disturbing. When two villagers had a falling out, the whole community would accompany them to a special enclosure, in whose center were two raised stones set in the earth at a certain distance from one another. Armed with small sacks of rocks, the enemies faced off from atop these stone-age pitching mounds and took turns hurling their projectiles at each other's head. The Guanches' aim was legendary, so deadly that the excitement of the contest came not from the combatants' striking each other but from seeing who was best able to dodge the rocks. Losing typically meant getting killed; naturally, there were plenty of bets on both sides. Maybe our own contemporary forms of violence—guzzling Diet Coke on night flights to Tokyo alongside the kid you had for kicks—provide a better way of settling things.

2:00 P.M. It took several moments of severe uneasiness before I realized that I'm hungry. I missed lunch because there was nobody here to ask me for a peanut butter and jelly sandwich. I've been married for quite a few years, long enough so that I can no longer remember any whole day when I was a bachelor. On top of that, I've now been a father for five years.

Not long ago, Cathy and our little boy traveled to the Midwestern plains for the eightieth birthday celebration of

27

one of her grandmothers. I don't recall why, but I had to stay home. In less than twenty-four hours I resumed the rhythm that I'd lost after our son was born: I worked all night and woke up in the middle of the afternoon. I ate a dozen doughnuts a day. When they returned home, the fruit in our bowls was swarming with flies and the milk had gone sour. I wonder if that's how all bachelors live. Do they ever cook themselves a nice chicken almondine or toss a Greek salad? I suppose that every time Odysseus ate a vegetable, during all those years he spent sleeping around, away from his wife and child, it counted as a Greek salad. But what does a bachelor do when faced with the endless horizon of a Saturday alone?

In the kitchen pantry I find a box of Froot Loops the size of a suitcase. A lot of it has already been eaten, making me think that it must be a daily staple for one of my brothers-in-law. Setting the box out on the table, I figure I can finish it off without leaving anybody malnourished: tomorrow morning, between the pool and breakfast, I'll have time to visit the supermarket and replace it before everybody gets up. By the time they're all out of bed I'll have already played soccer, outfitted Buzz Lightyear with his galactic armor, and read the paper from front to back while watching cartoons. With their tousled, matted hair and pasty mouths, the sleepy denizens of the house will be pouring themselves their first cups of coffee while I'll be ready to crack open my first beer.

My wife and son must have eaten lunch by now. Studying a chart of famous shipwrecks on the Outer Banks of North Carolina that I bought at a local souvenir shop, I imagine they must have already reached the bird sanctuary at Pea Island National Wildlife Refuge. I've honestly never understood the fascination of bird-watching, a pastime so dear to the gringo heart. I remind myself to make a note about the Froot Loops: I'd rather not have to face down any of my brothers-in-law in a stone-throwing duel.

4:30 P.M. Ancient history resembles the old Mother Goose nursery rhymes that are still used to help English-speaking children learn to read. Once upon a time those rhymes probably described political and social realities that everybody understood, but nowadays all such references have been lost. All we can do now is enjoy the cadences of a highly stylized imaginative code, preserved in print. And like Mother Goose rhymes, the chronicles of the conquest of the Canary Islands—by Cerdeño, by Gómez Escudero—make for good reading, but you can only take them in small doses. I'll opt for *The Odyssey* on the beach.

It's pretentious, I admit, taking such a high-caliber classic out to play in the sand. But it was meant to be. I usually travel with just one or two novels and a single book of poetry, but on this trip I couldn't avoid bringing a huge load of material for my work. Besides the volumes I checked out on the history of the Fortunate Isles, I've also got—I'm a professor of literature—volume one of the *Complete Works* of Martín Luis Guzmán. It's practically a solid cube—perhaps the most single difficult work in the history of literature to get into a suitcase.

I've been reading Guzmán at night and the historians when my son takes his nap. For going to the beach I scoured the anonymous selection of books that belong to this house. On other trips and in other cities I've found books that ended up profoundly affecting me, such as Julius Caesar's *Commentaries on the Gallic War* or *The Loss of El Dorado* by V. S. Naipaul. I was looking for some kind of detective thriller when I found the Penguin Pocket Classics edition of Homer and sat down to have a look at it. My son was watching *Bambi*. He asked me what kind of book could possibly distract me from such a movie—another kind of classic. I told him that it was about mermaids (not sirens)—that seemed to satisfy him. Later on he wanted me to tell him about the mermaids. I told him a fairly faithful version but made a few subtle changes; the mermaids still fed on sailors but I omitted the abundant sadomasochistic details of the original text. That's a good story, he replied, with a hint of menace in his voice. You can tell me the rest of it tonight. I got busy reading *The Odyssey* so that I'd have something else to tell him by bedtime.

5:00 P.M. Before settling down to read in the sand with all the quiet calm of my bachelor days, I walked along the beach. Staring out at the sea, I figured that by now my family must be on the ferry from Cape Hatteras to Ocracoke Island. It was those shallow waters that swallowed the ship of Blackbeard, last of the legendary pirates. In 1718, Edward Teach—his real name—was resting after one of his atrocious raids. Like all his forerunners, Blackbeard knew he would be left to his own devices as long as he laid low in the Carolina estuaries. That very fact enabled the British to set up a blockade. Two navy schooners launched a surprise attack against his ship, and their broadsides sent him to the bottom without much of a fight. My wife and son, and some of their relatives on today's outing, count among their ancestors the admiral who commanded the mission. It brought an end to piracy, once so lucrative for the English crown, but which political and economic developments had rendered obsolete.

As I walk along, I also think about Guzmán, quite possibly Mexico's best storyteller. He was also a man who found politics so tempting that he could only write during his periods of exile, when he had no other way to make a living except by writing. No writer is more deserving of Quevedo's oft-quoted praise of quietude, to which we professors at American universities—without a doubt the people in this world who work least for the most money—so proudly pay lip-service during our frivolous sabbaticals:

> Locked away in the peace of these deserts,
> With a small, learned gathering of books
> I live conversing with those expired
> My eyes listening to the resting dead.

Guzmán's periods of exile, like those of Quevedo, were authentic and obligatory. Both of them were men of action who were condemned, from time to time, to quiescence—a curse for which we, their readers, should be selfishly grateful. Sometimes I feel a bit like an exile, but for the most part I have to admit that I'm really nothing more than a high-class wetback.

My wife and son should have returned by now. If they get home any later we're going to have to go out for dinner.

8:35 P.M. I got back to the house a while ago. I went to the pool but no one else was there and it was terribly boring. I can't read either, I'm too worried that they're not back yet. I turn on the TV to catch the baseball game without anybody suggesting we change the channel and watch cartoons instead. I open the giant-size bag of Tostitos and pour a Diet Coke. The silence has become unbearable so I turn up the volume. The poet Julio Trujillo is right when he says that baseball is an Odyssean sport: the batter has to circle round the archipelago of the bases to get back home.

Between innings I step out onto the balcony. I see that all the neighbors who hate the ocean without realizing it have returned home. Now they're out taking walks to make their vacations tolerable. I wonder if my family's ship might have had engine troubles and sunk.

11:15 P.M. The game's finished. They still haven't gotten home or called.

1:00 A.M. I can't get to sleep. I take out the trash and check to make sure all the outside lights are on: maybe in the dark they couldn't recognize the house and just drove past. Coming back inside I see a sign above the door I hadn't noticed before: *Ithaca*.

HEAVY WEATHER

1. AIR

> Things out of order are restless; restored to order,
> they are at rest.

ST. AUGUSTINE, *Confessions*, XIII, 9

The first things that went flying by the window were newspapers and plastic bags. This wouldn't have been unusual for autumn, but we were sitting in a third-floor classroom at the time. We were talking about how Rubén Darío had been abandoned as a baby, and I interrupted the discussion to comment on the disgusting weather found on the East Coast of the United States. My students just sat there, staring back at me with hostility—for my own sanity I've decided that they always look that way—so I simply continued with my lecture. By now we were talking about Darío's arrival at Valparaíso, when something else went flying by the window; it might have been a tarp from a construction site, the hood of a car, or a calf. Instantly, the Wizard of Oz file in my mind clicked open and I proposed that we head downstairs to the basement and finish class in one of the lecture halls there. They followed my instructions—for the first time—with military discipline.

The Foreign Languages building where I teach usually empties out around three o'clock each afternoon. The hallways end up littered with garbage, like in the aftermath of a summary execution: open notebooks, disposable cups rimmed with lipstick traces, a sweatshirt or cap flung into the corner. The hastily abandoned classrooms exude the same feeling one must get while staring at the charred, smoking remains of a massacre. The whole place smells like a bombed-out city. To avoid further distractions, I chose a windowless classroom, and managed to get as far as Darío's move to Buenos Aires. I told them that as soon as the Nicaraguan poet stepped off the boat, the Spanish language was never the same, that the known world ended right then and there, and that another one—possibly better, but certainly different—began. Darío, I declared, in a rapture of lyricism that earned me a variety of odd looks, from hostile to confused, was the writer who'd flushed all the old crap down the toilet.

After that, we managed a fairly decent review of several of Darío's poems, with time still left for me to discuss the details of an assignment they had to turn in for the next class. As always, I thanked them for their patience. Nobody said you're welcome, so I figured they'd had enough of me.

After class, I took my time gathering up my papers and books to avoid running into one of my students at the bus stop or, later, on the Metro. I never really know what to say when I do. I feel as though I'm going to end up sounding like a pervert, no matter what I say. Adjusting my glasses on the bridge of my nose every few moments, I pretended to be absorbed with my roster. I briefly looked over my notes again and then, with exaggerated care, packed everything into my briefcase. I left the building only when I was sure they'd all melted away into the sprawling campus.

Outside it was odd to see no one sitting on the patio. Thanks to its comfortable tables in the shade right outside a building frequented by foreign exchange students, it's usually populated by packs of smokers. A heavy, humid breeze, more appropriate to August than the end of September, was stirring the astonishing amount of sodden trash left by the storm in the corners of the patio and all around the legs of the chairs. Then I heard the sound of sirens in the distance, and realized how uneasy I was already feeling.

Ever since the mournful days of the Mexico City earthquake in 1985, the sound of ambulances fills me with an anxiety that I'm always slow to identify. For the better part of two weeks, sirens provided the only soundtrack to our paralyzed lives. I'll never forget the mornings I spent as part of a team of senior high school students hauling and delivering food in Tepito, a neighborhood that had been completely destroyed. This is what Mexico City will look like when the gringos declare war on us again, El Pollo said to me. He was hard at work playing the role of emergency driver in the improvised ambulance we'd made out of his truck, sticking giant crosses of red tape to its sides. Afterward—as with Darío and tradition—nothing in Mexico was ever the same: we flushed the toilet on sixty years of half-assed tyranny. Although the older generations have a hard time accepting it, we had ourselves a real revolution, *a la* Hemingway: by carrying stretchers.

To get to the street that runs through the center of campus you have to traverse a long meadow bordered by oak trees. Normally this walk cheers me up when I've had enough of being an insignificant foreigner: teaching classes in Latin American literature at a gringo university is like cutting trees in a deserted forest with no one around to hear them fall. As I walked, I felt increasingly sure that something ominous was afoot: not a soul in sight on the paths, and the whining sirens were growing more intense as I approached the university's main road. At that point I was still sufficiently unaware of events to be annoyed by the idea that, whatever had happened, the road would be clogged with terrible traffic and I'd end up taking forever to reach the Metro. I checked my pocket and made sure I had enough change to call my wife from a pay phone. I wanted to let her know that she should go ahead and give the kids dinner. I'd be home as soon as possible.

Which turned out to be the last ordinary worry I'd have, that evening: I got to the main drag only to find it closed off and deserted. The bus stop was encircled by yellow police tape. The ambulances sounded farther away now. Seized by a ferocious dread, I walked toward the student commons where the cafeterias, bookstores, and post office were located. All deserted. I walked the hallways, climbing and descending staircases. Everything was closed and lonely. In the main dining room the tables were covered with dozens of abandoned meals: half-eaten hamburgers, full cups of soda, plastic spoons navigating melted sundaes. At the reception desk, I rang the visitors' bell over and over in a sort of hysteria.

Before going back outside and starting my long walk to the Metro station—I'd had to do the same thing once before, when a snowstorm shut down bus service while I was busy in the library—I stopped at a bank of pay phones to call my wife and ask her what was going on. The line was dead. Then I heard the unmistakable sound of a whole crowd of people walking together in silence.

I ran upstairs and came face to face with a huge line of students shuffling along in a tight, orderly, disciplined column, following a volunteer wearing a florescent orange vest over his everyday clothes. In the crowd, I recognized a woman from Panama who was a former student of mine. I pulled her out of line and asked her what was going on. There was a tornado, she told me in a stupefied voice that seemed to come not from her throat but from somewhere deep inside her.

What happened? It hit the dorms by the football stadium. I felt a new surge of fear: the university nursery school, which my children attended, was in the same complex of buildings. What time had it happened? I asked her. She wasn't sure. I'd just come out of psychology class, she said, and they locked us inside the first-floor classrooms. I was on my way to my next class, it must have been about four o'clock, right now they're rounding everybody up because there's another one coming. But the rest of the school's deserted, I told her. They're underground, she said, they've got half the university in the basement.

Without saying good-bye I ran toward the outer doors. Another volunteer blew his whistle when he saw me go past. I ignored him: Cathy picked up the kids at five o'clock, which meant they would have been evacuated with everybody else.

I often had to swing by and grab the kids when my wife's job at that insurance company required her to work into the evening. I also had transportation duty on Fridays, which was my only day off. The nursery school—a low, wide building, with a tornado watchtower on the roof—was located on the flattest, most open part of the campus, between the sports complex and some Soviet-style dorms that provided cramped housing for most of the undergraduates. When there was bad weather—in this country it's always either too hot or too cold, or it rains or floods or freezes or hails—I'd take the campus loop bus; otherwise, I'd make the half-hour walk, generally arriving late. The principal would greet me with a reproving stare, all her stereotypes about Mexicans confirmed as I came through the door dripping sweat, a good ten or fifteen minutes past closing. In the three years

37

my kids had spent at the school, the only expression I'd ever seen on her, even when I arrived on time, was that of the Protestant matron enraged at the world's immorality.

The day of the tornado I covered the last five hundred or thousand yards by cutting across lawns and meadows. The police had all the roads and sidewalks blocked off and I didn't want them to pick me up for evacuation before finding out if the kids had been taken to a safe location in time. The damage got worse as I neared my destination, going from upsetting to catastrophic. I finally found my way blocked by a massive tangle of uprooted trees and chunks of asphalt; the only way forward was to scramble over it all. An entire lamppost had been plucked from the ground and coiled like a corkscrew around the trunk of an oak tree. The image of that hideously twisted metal is burned into my memory, I fear, forever.

The street leading to the nursery school's front entrance was blocked by cars crushed by fallen trees. I was clambering over the debris when I felt someone grip my shoulder. It was a policewoman in full riot gear. She shouted at me that the whole area was off limits. I realized then that I'd managed to tune out the hellish racket of sirens and hammering combined with the sound of the wind, which was starting to pick up again now. I pulled away from the woman without answering, but only made it a few yards before she caught me again. I told her my kids had been inside when the tornado hit. Everybody was very worried, she said, but she could not, unfortunately, let me through. I asked if she'd heard about any victims. She said there were some casualties but didn't know how many or if any were from the school. The children and teachers had all been evacuated to the sports complex. This time I escaped by scrambling over the roof of a car, but in a few moments she collared me again, twisting my right arm up behind my back. She threatened to arrest me if I tried running again, and in that case I certainly wouldn't find out about my children any time soon. She frog-marched me away and turned me over to a volunteer with a blond crew cut who weighed at least 450 pounds. Without releasing my arm he more or less carried me into the gymnasium. I remember scanning the scene in desperation and noticing that the whole roof had been peeled off the daycare building. My last sight of the emergency zone was two firefighters cutting open a car to remove the passengers, their only available light cast by the spinning beacons on nearby rescue vehicles.

Gringos are an obedient sort of people: in full compliance with the authorities they were now organized into assigned groups and distributed throughout the gigantic subterranean sports complex. The ground floor, with its swimming pools under glass domes, was off-limits. The huge volunteer dumped me into a human river flowing downstairs to the lower levels. I asked a number of people if they knew the whereabouts of the kids from the nursery school, but nobody had news.

I left the spiral stairway on the first floor below ground level and went looking for the gymnasiums. Large tribes of young people seated in big circles were playing cards or talking and shouting to one another. One group told me they had seen a woman with a bunch of little kids on the basketball courts on the fourth floor, two more flights down.

As soon as I got back into the river of people heading downstairs, I noticed that the lower levels were much warmer: the electricity must have been knocked out; what little power we still had was thanks to the university's generator. That explained why there was no air conditioning. The crowd advanced slowly, like a mob of sleepwalkers.

The basketball courts filled an immense cavern. All the times I had made the walk to the nursery school, I'd never imagined that such a space existed beneath my feet. Students were camped out in groups, reading, sleeping, or doing homework. A volunteer signaled to me, index finger raised to his lips, that it was forbidden to make noise there. I couldn't imagine that they would try to keep children there, under such conditions, so I kept moving.

In the hallway I ran into a Korean professor of economics I knew, an acquaintance from some of the Fathers' Nights at the nursery school. He was leading his son by the hand so I latched onto his coattails and asked him where the other kids were. At first he looked disconcerted, as if staring at me from inside a thick bubble. Then he seemed to recognize me. In one great rush he began to give me a scattered account of how a falling tree had smashed the hood of his car. He and his kid had waited quietly inside until the storm passed and then run to the school, which by then had had its doors ripped off and windows shattered, and was missing part of its roof. He kept saying that he didn't know what he was going to do: he had just bought a house, and his insurance wouldn't pay for the car because he hadn't gotten any coverage for Acts of God. It took some effort to snap him out of it so that he could give me some more pertinent details: everyone at the school had been evacuated, they were in the women's locker room down on the lowest level. It was pretty dark down there, he said, and really hot, so he was looking for someplace to buy his son a cold drink.

I headed downstairs, leaving him to his monologue about the irrationality of a culture that attributes natural phenomena to God, as if he were chief clerk in charge of the weather. Past the fifth level it grew noticeably darker: only a few lights were on, and the red emergency lights gave the place a twilight atmosphere. The heat was so intense that there were only a few students still moving around.

As I stepped off the spiral stairway on the seventh level I discovered all the university students—male and female—stripped down to their underwear, seated on benches, and chatting away as if it were the most normal thing in the world. Down here there was no adult supervision. The sheen of their bare shoulders, stomachs, and legs made me realize that I was completely soaked in sweat.

I hurried to one of the locker rooms, bolting through the door with all the violence of my mounting desperation. Inside, the dense, acrid air reeked with a purely human decay. As I moved along the hallway leading to the lockers and showers, I thought it was an absolute disgrace to have banished the nursery children down here; they should have been upstairs where there was fresh air. The light, too, was awful, with only those sinister red emergency lights glowing on the tiles.

I reached the end of the hallway and turned the corner, but instead of children and their teachers I found dozens of naked bodies, all intertwined, pulsing and grinding together on the floor and benches, and even propped up next to the lockers. Like some divine beast gestating and multiplying, it writhed and flowed in slow motion, some part of each body gripping and being gripped by the hands, mouth, sex, or ass of another. Their pale torsos in the red light reminded me of the tin cans filled with earthworms that we used to collect in my grandmother's garden in Autlán before going fishing.

I stood there paralyzed by the liquid mass of bodies, completely absolved for a moment of my personality and private anguishes. One of the young men whom I had seen chatting outside came walking past me. He was just about to lose himself inside the soft, pulpy turmoil when I came to my senses and ran to grab his arm: I asked him about the nursery school kids. He told me he didn't know, he had just been on the tennis courts at the fifth level; there were no kids there. Let me ask, he said at last. He gestured for me to wait and approached a nearby group of bodies, all molded tightly together. They spoke among themselves without stopping work on each others' interlocking parts. At last one young woman slipped a penis out of her mouth and told me that all the kids were in the women's locker room, which was on the other side of the stairs.

Feeling drowsy and overwhelmed by the poor lighting, lack of oxygen, and the accumulated shocks I'd suffered, I walked toward the women's locker room with the lassitude of a man resigned to his fate. I had to knock on the door and identify myself before they would open up and let me in. Once inside, one of the teachers apologized, saying that they'd had to lock themselves in. When all the students began stripping off their clothes, they'd sent a father and his son to find help, but they hadn't returned. I didn't tell her that I had run into them enjoying a floor with fresher air. Instead, I went directly past the lockers until I could hear the sounds of children playing as though nothing unusual were happening.

Before arriving where they'd been corralled—the kids were sitting in a circle, surrounded by fans—I came face to face with another father, a Colombian man with whom I often chatted. He was distracted, staring at the floor with his hands in his pockets, and didn't notice me until I said his name. He looked in my eyes and for a fraction of a second didn't recognize me, then I saw a flash of fear cross his face. Didn't Cathy manage to get out? he asked. I don't know, I answered. I saw her leaving with your kids when I was coming in, he told me. The tornado hit when I was signing out

Jorgito. He ran his fingers through his sweaty mop of hair. Struggling to compose himself, he sent me off to talk to the principal who was further inside.

All the teachers went silent when they saw me standing there. Aren't Cathy and the kids with you? the principal asked without getting up from the bench where she was sitting. She opened the gigantic purse she always carried and took out her mobile phone, handing it straight to me. Call your house, she told me—maybe she was already safe when all hell broke loose.

Cell phones were still a novelty in those days: once I had it in my hands I didn't know how to use it. She told me I had to punch in the number then press the green button, but that to get a signal I had to go upstairs, as close to the ground floor as possible; down below, here among the furnaces and heating ducts, there was no way to get through to anybody. The pained looks that followed me as I made my way out of there made it completely clear: none of them harbored the least hope that my family had made it home before the tornado struck.

With more resignation than anguish, I walked back through the outlandish scene in the hallway. Now it came to me that I had needed to go to the bathroom for ages now, but all the pent-up tension in my body had prevented me from paying this any mind. Not wanting to run into another orgy, I went up to the next floor to find a men's room. I had to wait in a long line to take a crap in an overtaxed toilet. As I flushed, I had my first clear inkling that I might well no longer have a family; that my whole emotional universe had been shot to hell while I was reading a handful of poems by Rubén Darío that none of my students would ever remember.

I walked on upstairs, no longer in any hurry, thinking

over, for example, how difficult it was going to be to break the news to my parents that I was suddenly a widower and their grandchildren were no more. When I reached the spot where a phalanx of volunteers blocked the way up to the surface, I was already feeling the first stirrings, inside me, of an unexpected sense of freedom.

I punched in the number for my house and nobody picked up, not even the answering machine: the power was out. I dug around in my briefcase, looking for my in-laws' phone number. They live farther away from campus, so their electricity was probably still working. I dialed and my wife answered. In a perfectly relaxed voice she asked if the lights had come back on at home yet. She said she'd left me a note on the table explaining how she couldn't cook anything so she'd taken the kids to have dinner at her folks' house. I told her where I was calling from. She simply couldn't believe it. Yes, she'd noticed how strongly the wind was blowing when she left the school but she'd made if off campus without any problems. In the car they'd been listening to a tape of children's music, and at her parents' house they'd put on a cartoon video, so she had no idea what was going on. We agreed that they should spend the night there. That way she would be able to pick me up in the car when the authorities finally allowed us to leave. I had to control my voice so that she wouldn't pick up on how annoyed I was.

Back downstairs—the cell phone burning in the palm of my right hand—I stopped at the bottom of the stairway. The question was, should I go into the women's locker room or the men's?

2. Natural Disasters Recorded Since I Moved to Washington, D.C.

Three tornados.
An eighteen-month drought.
Six ice storms.
Hurricanes Isabel, Cecilia, and Laura.
Two floods on the Potomac from winter thaws.
Three complete closures of the city due to snowfall.
Threat of anthrax contamination.
A jetliner crashing into the Pentagon.
One divorce.

Thy gift sets a spark within us and we are raised up.
Our souls ablaze, we walk forward on the path.

ST. AUGUSTINE, *Confessions*, XIII, 9

It was the end of August. I had developed the annoying habit of brooding over the storms of volcanic ash that covered Mexico City with thick gray dust during the last spring that I lived there. In those days, when we were preparing to move from D.F. to D.C.—that is, from the *Distrito Federal* to the District of Columbia—I thought that the ashes were some kind of message from on high, urging me to get out. Now I understand that they were rather more admonitory in nature, but this realization only comes now, as I sit here writing, sketching out such a pleasant yet constricted scene, which has nothing to do with the disjointed flow of reality. Telling a story means tracing your finger through the ashes left by the fires of experience: the touchstone of all tragedy is our inability to remember the future.

Midsummer in the District of Columbia brings some of the most intense, sweltering weather in the northern hemisphere. Between July and August there are days when you can't even wear rubber-soled shoes because they start to melt the moment you set foot on the pavement. Unlike in other latitudes, the first whisper of autumn comes not with the crisp northerly breezes of October but instead with the heavy rain clouds left by hurricanes in the Gulf of Mexico at the end of August and beginning of September.

That morning we decided to take a bicycle ride down

to the airport. It makes for a quiet family outing. It's been years since weekends have felt the least bit restful: running the gauntlet of all the arbitrary, obligatory leisure activities here is even more exhausting than the hardest days at work. However, the ride out to the National Airport has its rewards. Cyclists are treated to a lengthy stretch along the banks of the Potomac. There is also the intensely strange experience of picnicking in the park that the airplanes fly over just before they land. The park's meadow is so close to the landing field that the planes fill the sky as they descend, drowning out all other sound as they pass within a stone's throw.

The clouds looked like solid steel, but as the seasons change they frequently remain that way for days on end without raining a drop. We set out around ten in the morning and followed our normal route: from the house to the playground around the corner, and from there along the path to Rock Creek Park, the spine of the city. There we stopped so that the kids could climb and swing and bounce.

It hadn't rained for several weeks, so the benches where my wife and I sat were covered with a fine layer of grit, an automatic reminder of the ashes from Popocatépetl in Mexico City seven years earlier. I mentioned this to Cathy but she told me that those ashes had a different consistency, with larger granules. She remembered when they first covered the windows of our apartment in Coyoacán; she had tried to brush them off with her hand but they stuck to her fingers. Everything's like that in Mexico, she said: tougher, harder to shake off.

Although it was hot and the humidity was outrageous—as always, in the summer—a southerly breeze made the second leg of the trip pleasant as we cycled to the zoo. We rode along in quasi-military formation: Cathy in the lead keeping an eye out for any obstacles, then our two kids on their mountain bikes, and me covering the rear of the pack to make sure no one got left behind.

We ate lunch at an open-air restaurant. Before continuing our ride, Cathy and the children visited the primate exhibit. As usual, I stayed outside to have a smoke: the chimpanzees and gorillas in their glass boxes reminded me too much of myself: despite being in exile, they lived a better life, now safer and better fed than in the miserable forests where they'd been captured. When we got back on the bike paths, the sky was already painted like an ominous stage scrim. The breeze was picking up, turning into wind. We considered the situation while we struggled to help the kids strap on their bike helmets. Since we were already closer to the river than home, we figured it was better to keep going. If necessary, we could always take the Metro back from downtown.

The truth is that we continued our outing only at my insistence: Cathy's memory of how the ashes from Popocatépetl clung to our hands when we tried to clean them off made me think of my grandmother—her ashes were the stickiest I've ever encountered. I felt for some reason that riding into the wind would cleanse my conscience of them.

My father's family, from whom I surely inherited my habit of constantly moving around—from one house, country, or spouse to another—has deep roots in the teaching profession: to this day, many of my relatives live likewise peripatetic lives, off in countries where producing or reproducing knowledge is actually a well-respected job. Several years ago, my paternal grandmother made the stupid mistake of dying suddenly, and on Holy Thursday eve, in the rather remote village of Autlán. Because one of her sons, and several grandchildren, were unable to make travel arrangements in time to attend the funeral Mass, it was decided to postpone the interment of her ashes in our family crypt until the following Monday. I managed to arrive on Saturday afternoon, just in time for the cremation. I also got to witness the very strange moment when my father and my uncles, after arguing about whether it was better to leave the ashes in the car until the ceremony began, or else bring them inside the house, finally decided on the latter. With a discomfort bordering on the ridiculous, they placed the urn on the sideboard by the table as if it were going to preside one last time over a family meal. It was decided by everyone that the youngest of us cousins would sleep in the house. Not having grown up there, we wouldn't find it so depressing to spend the night and stand the final watch.

It's not often that my family has so many relatives gathered under one roof, as we were that night under our grandmother's. The mournful atmosphere in the room, still so heavy when we sat down at the table, receded after the first couple of whiskeys, especially because more relatives kept knocking on the door, sometimes simply to pay their respects and sometimes because they were just arriving from the bus station. Our vigil didn't exactly turn into a party, not quite, but considering both the occasion and the fact that the ashes of its guest of honor were in attendance, the night was surprisingly relaxed.

Around midnight, or maybe one in the morning, my father and his brothers said goodnight, and headed over to our relatives' houses to sleep. It was then that my sister, Nena, raised her eyebrows at me with a conspiratorial look. She glanced toward the sideboard where my grandmother's ashes had stood watch over the excessive number of cocktails drunk in her honor.

The door had barely closed behind the older mourners

when all of us cousins who had stayed behind made an urgent—and frankly ridiculous—dash for the urn. We all held back a moment until Nena herself, the devious ring-leader of our riskiest childhood expeditions, stepped forward. She placed the urn on the table and removed the lid, revealing the deep, terrible void within. Suspended in a hallowed silence, we reverently gathered our heads around the receptacle as Nena reached her hand inside. She withdrew a fistful of our grandmother's remains and held them on her outstretched palm. They were not, as we had imagined, like the fine dust left behind after burning wood or paper; they were shiny little black stones, like pellets of obsidian, and we all crowded together to touch them. It was then that we discovered just how sticky they were: once you had some of Grandma's ashes on your fingertips there was no way to remove them. We ended up shaking and brushing off our hands over the urn—with pretty lousy aim—and at last had to remove the tablecloth and toss it into the garbage with my poor grandmother stuck all over it. Upon returning to D.C. I told Cathy all about it. In a rather serious voice, she told me that when she died I'd better not invite Nena to her funeral.

The descent to the Potomac was, at the very least, enjoyable: the cool steady wind blew straight into our faces as we rode down along the riverbanks. Also, we could ride without stopping: the kids still had all their energy, and nowhere on the route is there an uphill stretch that isn't preceded by an even longer descent, so you never have to get off and walk or push your bike. By the time we were approaching Watergate and had the river in sight, every cell in my body felt refreshed, as if I had been scrubbed clean.

Riding a bicycle is more a state of mind than hard work. Although it hurts at first to stretch your muscles and get warmed up, once the lungs and legs naturally and miraculously sync up, the body works automatically. Unless some sudden change in the terrain requires a shift in speed, there's no need to stop and rest. Though the banks of the Potomac slope downhill on the Capitol side—D.C. is built on swamps that once served as a drainage for Appalachian thaws—on the Virginia side they're as flat and green as soccer fields. We crossed the bridge, skirted Arlington Cemetery, and followed the riverside path toward the airport.

Before we even reached our destination, though, the sky began to roil and erupt. The storm hit with such violence that we heard it before anything else: we were by now very close to the landing field. When the lightning flashes and exploding thunder announced an imminent cloudburst, we stopped beneath one of the freeway bridges with another group of cyclists and some runners who'd also been counting on those imperturbable, late-season cloudbanks. Cathy took our picnic blanket out of her backpack while I removed sodas, olives, and potato chips from the cooler in my basket. We spread out our little sheltered camp and from there we watched the river churning with the rainfall in the distance until the storm front reached the bridge.

Although we got a bit chilly—rain always carries an icy presence that clings to your shirt with all the tenacity of human ashes—we entertained ourselves by calculating how far away the lightning was striking: reason is the only human defense against our primal fear of the elements. At one point the rain was so heavy that we couldn't even see the river, which was barely ten yards away from our picnic blanket.

The storm passed as nimbly as it arrived. We had finished our olives and were still nibbling on potato chips when a small but promising ray of sun broke through the clouds.

Children—like Mexico, like ashes—are sticky: for parents, some ridiculously simple tasks, like getting into the car or choosing a movie at the video store, become endless, herculean tasks. The runners and other cyclists sheltering beneath the bridge had long ago returned to the path when we felt ready to resume riding with all our gear, once more in strict formation.

We had only gone a few hundred yards when I became aware that my bicycle and I had penetrated into a different reality, as though we were at the center of a cone of silence. I looked ahead at Cathy and the kids and saw their faces distorted by a spasm of fear: whatever was going on, it was happening only to me. Looking down, I saw a glowworm devouring my handlebars in slow motion. As it touched my hands, they turned the very shade of blue they'll become when I'm dead. My wedding ring, on my right hand, flared molten green. In spite of the intense pain produced by the burning ring, I couldn't let go of my bicycle: my body was trapped in a surging vibration, as if a magnet was drawing me up by the hair to some paradise I don't deserve. I'm dying, I thought. Cathy and the children were shouting something at me—who knows what—from the world of sound they still inhabited. In return I gave them a smile more resigned than sad.

Then thunder shattered the silence. It wasn't the usual deafening sound as it might be heard by ears outside my electric womb, but a soft, precise crack, like a handclap. Still, I was able to see the two trees nearest the path get blown to pieces before collapsing in clouds of smoke. Blackened and burning from the lightning, their limbs fell around me in a perfect circle. Dismounting from my bicycle I sensed, for the first time in my life, the astonishing firmness and solidity of the ground. I touched one of the branches and felt its embers burn my fingertips. Hoisting my bike to my shoulder, I removed the leaves, bark, and branches, and checked to make sure it was all in one piece. Then, despite having been just struck by lightning, I proposed that we keep riding toward the airport.

Once we reached the meadow we were disappointed to see that the stormy weather had forced a change in the runway patterns. Now we couldn't watch the planes landing. Instead, as we lay on our backs in the wet grass, we could only see their departures, which are always anticlimactic.

Saving Face

TOILET

... gentle fatherland, pantry and aviary.

RAMÓN LÓPEZ VELARDE

It was Sunday and Jordan Marcus was peering out the window of his fourth floor apartment at the corner of 15th and Fuller. The telephone rang. He was wearing a T-shirt, elbows resting on the windowsill, hoping for a breeze off the Potomac that wasn't going to blow till autumn. Methodically scanning the row of windows in the building across the street, he checked on his neighbors as though they were birds in cages. Over the years, with patient effort, he had been able to glimpse some fabulous, indeed lubricious, scenes within the shadows of those apartments. On the fourth floor, the same little old insomniac lady who was always there stood with her face pointed at the rising sun; her burned-out eyes, long-covered with cataracts, staring opaquely from behind Coke-bottle lenses. Lower down, to the left, a fat man dunked bread into his coffee, tits slipping out from behind his tank top. The other apartments were still dark or had their blinds lowered.

A woman's voice reached his ears, distorted by the grating noise of the fan blowing hot air onto the back of his neck. It's for you, she said. What. The telephone. What telephone. The phone, they're calling you about some emergency. Marcus got up from his chair slowly, taking advantage of the angle afforded by standing to steal one last look at the windows across the way, then turned back into the apartment and walked down the sky-blue hallway. He'd painted it that color during one of the ferocious bouts of perfectionism that periodically drove him to lead a more dignified life. He didn't bother getting the phone in the kitchen where it was waiting off the hook: the receiver was so greasy that it always slipped from his fingers in the muggy heat. In the living room—painted green in an earlier outburst of energy—he plopped onto the couch with a sigh, as he did every night to watch TV after the last curtain was drawn in the building across the street. Using the hem of his shirt to wipe the sweat off his face, he picked up the receiver. Hello? The answer was drowned out by the sound of bacon sizzling in a frying pan. Just a moment please, he said. Covering the mouthpiece, he shouted at the woman to hang up, that he'd picked up. He waited for the line to quiet down to ask what the matter was. A polite voice with an Hispanic accent apologized for calling him so early, but the electricity was off and needed to be repaired before eight A.M. He'd been recommended, the caller said, because he lived near the restaurant, and they needed power before the first customers showed up. Which restaurant? Marcus asked. Guadalupe's, at 13th and Harvard. They told me it's not too far from your house. Only three blocks, Marcus answered. He excused himself for a moment to check his work orders for the day, then just sat for a moment on the couch, the receiver muffled against his belly. He scratched his scraggly beard with his free hand and thought about his captive birds in the building across the street. When he figured that a reasonable amount of time had passed, he answered: I'm gonna have to cancel a job I've got at eight-thirty.

In the kitchen, his woman was at the stove frying eggs. I have to go out, Marcus told her, right now, and he poured himself some coffee. It's an emergency. She turned away from the stove to stare at him, then set down the spatula on the stovetop, and put her hands in the pockets of her pink terrycloth robe: in the four or five months they had been together, she'd never seen him in a hurry.

He ate his breakfast standing up, then clattered the plates into the dishwasher. Going to his bedroom he took his coveralls out of a closet with missing doors. His clothes smelled like mildew. He picked up yesterday's socks from the floor and sat down by the window to get ready. All the while, slipping on one sock, then another, and then the coveralls, he kept looking out the window for some freshly opened curtain. He put his boots on, carefully snugging the laces at each turn. He was working on the second boot when something moved in the building across the street. Dickey bird, he thought, and froze, keeping his eyes riveted to the spot until he felt sure the blind wasn't going to go up after all. Back in the hallway he paused to take his toolbox out of the linen closet where it was buried between packages wrapped in polyethylene bags. He was about to leave without saying good-bye when the woman grasped his arm. Well? she asked. What? What's the big hurry? It's an emergency. And since when do you accept emergency jobs? Don't I bring home enough money for you? I've never been inside Guadalupe's he said, slamming the door.

Marcus stepped decisively from his building's vestibule, then recoiled as he turned to walk north. He took courage from waving hello to some of the neighbors. They were still awake, reeking of sweat, sitting out on their front stoops where they'd been lazily talking all night long. He'd stopped going north of Fuller Street after the Hispanics began moving into that part of the neighborhood. To get to the Metro now he would normally head south a few blocks and then turn and walk back north by way of 12th Street, no-man's-land. He'd also changed supermarkets, and now shopped at one farther away which didn't sell such strange, monstrous fruit.

The Cuban exiles from the Mariel Boatlift were the first birds to land, basking in the glow of positive press; and there had been a certain romance to the new and different smells on the street. Then came the Dominicans, the Salvadorans, the Ecuadorians, and the Peruvians. In the last few years the Mexicans had shown up: the gringos' evil twin.

He shook hands with the filthiest of his neighbors and then headed up the street. He crossed Fuller without looking to either side. Staring at the ground, he passed by the building on the opposite corner as fast as he could. He was walking like someone who doesn't want to be recognized, but there was nobody sitting in the doorway. It might have been the sticky August heat, or the memory of his birds in their shadows, but the faster he walked the more trapped he felt. It was the same feeling he'd had as a boy, if it was getting late and he took a shortcut home through the muddy backstreets to avoid a beating from his father, the pastor. He'd always been, and still was, the black sheep of the family. The third son of a Baptist minister, Marcus was the only bad apple. Still walking north, he quickened his step and thought that the Spanish he heard spoken beyond Fuller—so lacking in consonants—sounded like pigeons cooing. He was out of breath by the time he reached the corner of Harvard. Turning east he found that he didn't recognize the street. In another lifetime, before going to prison, before the Cubans, he'd had a steady girlfriend from this neighborhood. She'd lived in one of the stone houses on the left side of the street but he couldn't remember exactly which one. In those days, now faded and all but forgotten, the pastor still believed that Marcus might be reformed. He didn't have to walk much further before he could make out the sign on

Guadalupe's up ahead. He covered the last stretch almost running, the toolbox knocking against his knee.

It's not that Marcus had turned out to be bad, not exactly, but he had never been able to rise to the pastor's expectations. So he had early on succumbed to the notion that any flaw or weakness in himself meant that he was, as a whole, irredeemable. During the four years of his first prison stint no one ever came to visit him, not once. Even so, he spent his time thinking of going home, about regaining his dignity by playing the role of the prodigal son.

They let him out on an icy Friday in February. To better stage his dramatic return to the world of the living, Marcus spent his first two nights in a hotel, waiting to appear at his father's church during Sunday services. In order to proclaim his rebirth as loudly as possible, he paid more than he could afford for a brand new blue suit. On Sunday he arrived at the church ahead of schedule, then hid out in a café, killing time so the whole congregation would be there to witness his return. As they were singing the opening hymns he came walking up the aisle with a slow, humble step dogged by the worshippers' murmuring. He sat down just a few rows from the altar, in the pews opposite those occupied by his mother and brothers, his sisters-in-law, his older nephews, and the children born while he'd been away. Before the pastor appeared to deliver his sermon from the pulpit, one of the ushers was sent to escort Marcus out of the church.

The front door to Guadalupe's was still locked, so Marcus went round to the service entrance and knocked hard. He was already soaked in sweat and hadn't even started working yet. It must have been about a year now since his last outbreak of perfectionism; he remembered painting his room canary yellow one day during an equally unpleasant heat wave. When he'd come back to the apartment with the can of paint, the young girl who was turning tricks for him at the time was asleep. He punched and slapped her awake and, in no time at all, had kicked her out with all her belongings. Then he cleaned the corners, emptied out the closet, pushed all the furniture into the center of the room, and covered it all with a sheet. He finished painting the four walls quickly and thought that he might continue with the kitchen. Instead, while the first coat dried, he got a chair out from under the sheet and sat down to do some bird-watching. The bedroom was impeccable for half the afternoon— floor mopped, furniture dusted, window washed—but then he didn't have the strength to continue. All the satisfaction he required came from observing his neighbors' squalor from a sterile vantage. He called the contractor to let him know he was ready to take on some new jobs.

Although he wasn't wearing a watch, he knew from the angle of the sun that it was no longer so early, so he knocked harder. The door opened abruptly. A young woman—slight shoulders, sinewy arms and legs—stared out at him with a confused mixture of surprise and fear. She said something to him in Spanish. Marcus thought he could probably pick her up off the ground with one hand. In English, he said that he had come to fix the electricity. She told him to come inside, that her husband would be right back. He stroked his scraggly beard, bit his lower lip, and crossed the threshold with professional resolve.

He found the semidarkness inside the restaurant quite disorienting. A silent tremor shook the air and something moved among the furniture. The woman noticed that he was uneasy. It's the kids, she told him, then shouted at them in a threatening voice. They instantly bolted for the stairs and he only managed to get a good look at the last one: about ten years old, barefoot, shorts, no shirt—a long scrawny torso like a plucked chicken. The woman screamed at them again and their laughter answered from a back room. Then she led Marcus to the dining room and showed him the fuse box. The cooks get here at eight-thirty, she said. See if you can fix the problem before then. I'll be upstairs if you need me.

The restaurant fit the typical TV image he'd gotten of Mexico: large windows, bright colors, mismatched tables. The relative familiarity of the place allowed him to concentrate on the job at hand. He dismantled the fuse box, checked the circuit, and quickly located the socket causing the short. Working very calmly, he isolated the zone, replaced the burned-out pieces, upgraded the wiring, and cleaned the insulators. Every so often he turned to look toward the door that led from the dining room to the house, with the hope of catching sight of some bird—any bird at all.

As the restaurant owner didn't return, and there was no one to keep an eye on him, he left the fuse box hanging open so that he could charge them for a second hour of service. He gathered up his tools, walked between the tables, looked out the windows, and scanned the inside of the empty kitchen leisurely through the porthole on the door. He thought that if he'd known that the job was going to be so easy he'd have bought himself a newspaper to have something to pass the time with. At last, he sat down at a table next to the restroom, facing the doorway in case anybody stuck their head in. He closed his eyes for a catnap, thinking that he could be doing exactly the same thing at home.

He was on the verge of falling asleep when he heard a very faint voice. It was calling, with a certain insistence, from inside the restroom. He got up and cracked the door open so that he could listen closely without seeing inside.

The voice, he confirmed, was speaking to him, and in Spanish. A chill ran down his spine and he broke out in a cold sweat. Yes? he asked in English. The voice said something else to him he couldn't understand. Then, with his heart in his mouth, he stuck his head inside. Whoever it was, he saw, was calling to him from inside the closed toilet stall. The tremulous voice could have belonged to anybody except a man. Probably a child. Yes? Marcus asked again. He didn't understand the answer, which now seemed to come from a young woman. He couldn't even say if it had spoken to him in English—he was too busy thinking that the rest of the family flock was back inside the house, a good distance away, and he was here alone, on the verge of glory. He touched the stall door with his fingertips and felt it give slightly; it wasn't bolted. He swallowed and asked again what the person needed. The voice, perhaps an old woman's, repeated in English that it needed napkins. He went out, got a handful of paper napkins from the counter, and went back inside. He steadied himself with his left hand on the upper part of the stall—he could see his own sweat dripping onto the paper napkin, and said: Here they are. The voice thanked him, said that he could pass them over the top. Still undecided, he rested his head against his forearm. A moment later, with his eyes closed, he raised the handful of napkins and felt them snatched out of his hand. He said, You're welcome, and spun around. He closed up the fuse box as fast as he could, grabbed his things and left the dining room. Before leaving the restaurant he shouted to the whole bunch of them that he'd be back later for his money.

The harsh sunlight now flooding Harvard Street was a tremendous relief. He thought that with the amount he was going to charge them, and the money he could squeeze out of his latest whore before he ran her out the door, he could buy himself a new suit and three cans of white paint, enough to redecorate his whole apartment.

OUTRAGE

Why do I want a life without honor
If I already bet everything I had?

A. Esparza Oteo

A highway can be like the high seas. The sun burning on your face, the fresh cleansing breeze in your lungs, your hands tightly gripping the rails along the steel deck, the rotten stench rising from the bilge. Drake Horowitz believed this for quite some time without being able to test it out for himself. Being the newest crew member aboard the *Outrageous Fortune*, he had to sit in the middle of the front seat, between Verrazano and the driver. Company regulations prohibited riding outside the cabin when the truck was moving at high speeds. So, with growing resentment, he stayed put, poring over the latest American League scores in the sports section of the *Baltimore Sun*. Drake leaned forward slightly to keep his head out of the way, hardly paying any attention to the two men as they chattered and gossiped, trading thoughts, comments, and insults.

The idea of christening the truck came from a photo in a *National Geographic* they fished out of a black plastic garbage bag. All sorts of things drifted to their ship in that way, as if following the course of a secret tide. Hefting the trash bag, fat Verrazano noticed the dead ballast of printed material inside. He weighed it a moment, raising and lowering the bag clenched in his fist, eyes narrowed, lips drawn tight. Then he dropped it to the ground and squatted down, prodding and squeezing the contents: Those sons of bitches think they can fool a man who's been collecting trash for fifteen years! he said to his coworkers. After every squeeze his expert nose pondered the smells emanating from the bag: They're magazines, he continued, recent issues, good condition, perfectly recyclable. He didn't throw the bag into the trash compactor. Later, as they were heading back to the plant, he opened the sack and saw that it contained shopping catalogs and issues of *National Geographic*. Nary a hint of pornography. The driver, who according to the company hierarchy held the rank of ship's captain, proposed that they file a formal complaint about the customer—not for violating the recycling rule, but because it was, well, unbelievable. The goddamned white man's hypocrisy! he said in a low, dense, cavernous voice. Verrazano snorted in disgust and let the bag tumble to the floor of the cab. Drake, who had already finished the sports section, grabbed one of the magazines and began to flip through it. During their lunch break he showed them the photo. They'd stopped at a park and were seated at a picnic table, sharing a package of fish jerky and some crackers. Look, he told them, south of the border they name their trucks. The picture showed a dump truck, its rear license plate frame inscribed with a Spanish phrase in red letters: *No Me Olvides*. The next day, before reaching their assigned neighborhood, Drake proposed that they write *Outrageous Fortune* on the truck's rear bumper. Verrazano agreed immediately; he liked the idea of a personalized workspace: his own car sported various decorations that made it unique and, in his eyes, elegant. The Captain didn't even turn to look at them while they discussed it. Drake pointed out that they could also attach a flag to the truck, a black one, he said. Verrazano thought the idea strange but ballsy. It took them weeks to persuade the old man to let them paint the name on. He finally gave in, provided they would quit asking for the flag: company regulations prohibited exterior fixtures and any hanging objects. Fat Verrazano tried one last time, reminding him that the flag would be black. Like your ass, he added. The Captain told him to shut up. If not, he was going to throw the rosary out the window that Verrazano'd had the nerve to hang from the mirror on their first run together.

On the day when Drake Horowitz finally tested out his theory that the highway can be like the high seas, and a garbage truck like a ship, the morning dawned—in defiance of every sailor's superstition—without auguries. The night before, Drake had gone out to a minor-league game with his brother and his nephews, who swung by the plant early to pick him up. He didn't call his wife to tell her that he'd be home late. In recent weeks, even the least disagreement set her off on such a loud and wild tirade that he frequently had to slap her to calm her down. And Drake was no wife-beater, by nature. In the car, his nephews asked him about their cousin, but Drake just shrugged his shoulders reluctantly and said that he'd decided to stay home with his mother. Drake's brother, who knew that the couple were going through a rough spell, gave him a few quick pats on the shoulder before starting the motor. They all said nothing on the way, the boys arguing now and then and their father shouting them into silence when they got on his nerves. During the game, Drake and his brother drank so much that the eldest boy began to get worried, and even tried whining and crying to get them to stop. When beer sales were cut off at the top of the eighth inning they drove to a biker bar just off the highway. The idea was to buy a case of beer and drink it together back at Drake's apartment— the boys could sleep in their cousins' room—but the place seemed so comfortable, and the drive back to the city so

68

long, that they preferred to stay put. After the first shot of bourbon, Drake's brother went out to take his boys a little bag of peanuts and the car keys so they could listen to the radio. Drake's memory of the night faded out a short while later.

He awoke alone, stretched out on a bench at his neighborhood basketball court, guilt-free and soaked in sweat. He rubbed his face and looked at his watch. Nearly five o'clock in the morning and it had barely cooled off during the night. He started walking home quickly, thinking it was going to be a brutally hot day; he had little more than half an hour to shower and eat something before Verrazano rang his doorbell.

The christening of the *Outrageous Fortune* was just another inoffensive oddity, one of the many that arise in a garbage man's infinitely tedious life. Horowitz had chosen a fine name for his galleon and the Captain thought it would do no harm to make it official. After he got used to the sign on the rear bumper, he began using the name himself. He'd noticed that overlooking Drake's whims helped the poor disgruntled fellow get on better with his job. His minor peculiarities were always pretty tolerable, like having to eat jerky and crackers when it was Drake's turn to bring lunch; or getting used to those nautical terms: *hatch* for door, *bridge* for driver's cab, *helm* for steering wheel, *locker* for glove compartment. They were inoffensive manias, at least compared to Verrazano's outright insanity: the fat man was just as likely to pick a fight with a police officer as start kicking over the garbage cans at a house if he thought they'd been improperly filled.

The garbage truck had always made Drake think of a ship. But one morning the previous autumn the tide had brought them a box of books, and since then the idea had gained an increasingly strong hold over his mind. He was tying the remains of some broken furniture on top of the truck when Verrazano froze in his tracks, hands dead at his sides, a look of disbelief frozen on his face. Who do these people think they are? he screamed. This has got to violate every regulation of trash collection in the United States. Busy as he was with his task, Drake hardly paid him any attention. Look at this, Horowitz. Books. Right here, in an open cardboard box. I can't believe it. Descending the poop-deck ladder, Drake suggested he just dump them in the trash compactor and leave it at that. Impossible, responded Verrazano. Just throw them in the back and forget about it. That's a crime, Verrazano bellowed. Why? What do you mean, why; it's perfectly recyclable paper. Besides, they're books. Kids in the inner city can't even go to school and rich people in the suburbs throw books in the garbage. Then take 'em to the library or file a complaint against this house for not recycling, Drake said. With spluttering bravado, the fat man declared he would do exactly that, then set the box down in the truck's cab. Now with lunch finished—his wife had prepared them a fantastic lasagna—calm, settled, and bored by the long return trip to the plant, Verrazano began to look through the contents of the box. He leafed through two or three books. One of them caught his attention. Look at this one, he said, showing it to Horowitz. I can't believe this: *Song of Myself*. So much pride can't be good for kids. Verrazano grabbed the book by its spine and flung it out the window. The other two laughed. He kept on digging through the box. Oh, please, he said after a while, look at this. He showed them a copy of *Junkie*. Now, that's just plain wrong. He repeated his prank, and this time scored a direct hit on a mailbox. Ugh, *A Doll's House*. That's for whores and stuck up bitches, and he sent it sailing with style, like a Frisbee.

Mexico City Blues. He snorted. Beaners. Fuck that shit. I'm throwing that one, said the Captain. Nope, replied Verrazano, because here's one especially for you, and he handed him a copy of *Heart of Darkness*. And this one's for Horowitz: *Drake in the Pirates' Era*. When they reached the plant all the books had gone out the window except the one about pirates. Drake began reading it that very night. Things at home were still going well then: there was less time for him and his wife to drink when he was busy reading for a few hours every night.

Such repose would have been impossible during that summer, when the highway was like the high seas. Verrazano thought it strange that Horowitz was already waiting for him—with a face like a castaway's—on the front steps of his building. Even more so that he didn't react when Verrazano parked his white Galaxie right in front of him: it wasn't the kind of car that went unnoticed. He strained to lean over and roll down the passenger-side window, then whistled loudly to get his attention. Drake waved at him and got up clumsily, like a deep-sea diver moving with slow, meticulous care along the ocean floor. He was wearing the same clothes as the day before. From inside the car, the fat man saw him listlessly open the back door and drop a large, canvas duffel bag onto the seat, much bigger than the one he normally carried. The plush velvet seat cushions barely muffled the loud, metallic clatter of the bag's contents. Are you going to play ball after work? Verrazano asked. No, said Horowitz. But you've got your bat in there, right? And my rifle. Sure.

Once outside the city, as on every morning, they chose a random street where they could steal a newspaper. We're in luck, said the fat man as he spotted the *New York Times* in its blue plastic bag lying in the front yard of a McMansion.

71

Out on the highway, they stopped for coffee at a gas station mini-mart. There, Drake told him what had happened.

When he got back to his apartment after spending the night, or part of it, on the neighborhood basketball court, he was still floating in that hazy serenity between drunkenness and hangover. It took a while for his clumsy hands to fish the keys out of his jeans pocket. Feeling a little dizzy as he tried to choose the right one, he stopped and rested his head against the door, which swung open under its weight. Although he knew right away that his wife had left him, he preferred to think that the door had been left unlatched by accident, and even thought about giving her hell when she woke up to make breakfast for their son. Drake went quietly into the kitchen and drank a glass of milk. As he closed the refrigerator he saw the Post-it stranded in the center of the door bearing the most laconic of farewells: *I'm gone.* He peeled off the little square note and read it a few more times, surprised that he felt nothing. Before going into the bathroom he went to make sure that his son hadn't been left behind. Drake wouldn't have known what to do with him.

He felt a surge of relief at finding himself alone. In the bathroom he turned on the hot water and sat on the toilet, waiting for steam to fill the room before getting into the shower. He'd always thought that breathing in steam had some curative effect. Suddenly he had to piss. Standing up, he lifted the toilet seat lid and saw a couple of condoms floating in the bowl. A burning wave of pain shot up from the base of his spine and surged through his whole body. He kicked over chairs, smashed dishes, flipped the kitchen table upside down. In the bedroom Drake found her robe thrown on the floor next to the foil condom wrappers; a man's bikini briefs were hanging on the bedpost. He thought of setting fire to them but then saw they belonged to a much bigger man. He dropped them on the floor and sat down on the bed, temples pounding, his brain reeling between rage and self-pity. He held his face in his hands, rubbing slowly. Then he noticed the smell. It took him only a few seconds to discover, in the dead center of the bed, a turd so large it could not have been made by a woman.

Verrazano's reaction to the tale was surprisingly cool. You say he took a shit in your bed? Horowitz nodded his head. He's got to be Arab, or Chinese. Why? Christians don't do things like that. Besides, he had bikini underwear. Real men wear boxers. They sat in silence. Drake slid down in his seat, sinking beneath the weight of his hangover, which was now beginning to assume oceanic proportions. They were driving along the county road leading to the plant. Verrazano had his left hand on the wheel and was stroking his beard with the right. After a while the fat man spoke up, sounding like he had solved a riddle: And you brought your rifle to kill her if we run into them. Horowitz shrugged his shoulders. I'd do the same, brother, concluded the other man, gently massaging the back of his companion's neck. Drake was so distressed that the gesture actually seemed comforting.

It wasn't even six-thirty yet but it was already hot. The hazy white sunlight bounced off the plant's polished concrete in a soft humid blur, shooting directly into the softest, most sensitive part of Drake's brain. Sweat trickled down, stinging his unshaved face. His wristwatch hand was shaking so much he had to hold it steady with the other just to read the time. He had ten minutes before they headed out for the day, so he walked to the bathroom. He threw up his coffee then furiously washed his face. As he stood there staring at himself in the mirror he recalled how his brother had foreseen the whole blowup. One Sunday afternoon they had gotten together at Drake's apartment to eat lunch and watch a World Series game. They were out on the balcony, drinking beers and grilling sausages. Their wives were in the kitchen, busy making salad. The boys, having fun before the pre-game show started, were playing on an outdated video game console Drake had found a few days earlier next to a trash can in a wealthy suburb. The Horowitz brothers were in a good mood, recalling their youthful escapades in the neighborhood where Drake—the youngest—continued to be stuck. It was all so pleasant—the fresh breeze, the deep blue sky, the clear sharp afternoon light—that Drake started talking. He told his brother how he had figured out the origin of his name; it came from an infamous English admiral. He went inside the apartment for a minute and came out with the biography of Sir Francis Drake and a telescope— possibly the only object in the whole house that he had paid for. His older brother left the sausages a moment to open the telescope and scan the building on the other side of the street. Drake asked him if their father had chosen his name with the famous pirate in mind. His brother collapsed the telescope and looked at the cover of the book. He turned back to the grill and said he had never heard of any Polish sailor—the most likely thing was that their dad had really meant to name him Derek. He was always so drunk, and so stupid, he must've spelled it wrong at the city clerk's office, he concluded. An hour later, as they sat in front of the TV— wives and kids at the park—the older brother said that it wasn't really his business, but he'd noticed that his sister-in-law was acting strange, like she was hiding something. What? asked Drake, alarmed. I don't know, he answered. Maybe she's pregnant again and she's afraid to tell you, or maybe she's looking for a job. He shrugged his shoulders. During the commercial break he went to the kitchen for a couple of beers. He returned to his chair and handed one to Drake. Then, in the most casual voice he could muster, he said: Y'know, that stuff about pirates is just weird, like you're tryin' to hide from something, like with that Batman costume you wouldn't take off after Dad walked out. Find some other job, something normal, where you don't spend your whole day sitting between a couple of retards.

Drake emerged from the bathroom and put on his coveralls in the locker room. He felt the weight of destiny in his duffel bag as he crossed the parking area. The Captain was already on board the truck, motor running. Verrazano was standing next to the open door, waiting for him with a smile. Cheer up, Horowitz, he told him, we've got a long hot day ahead of us. Drake slid in and felt the heat from the already warm forecastle seat beneath his buttocks. The fat man got in and secured the hatch. Drake reached into the duffel and pulled out his telescope: he extended it and pointed it straight ahead, muttering: Anchors aweigh.

The Captain shifted into first gear and got rolling. In spite of the ugly domestic shipwreck that Verrazano had already related to him, he felt sure that work and operations aboard the *Outrageous Fortune* would go smoothly. The mood inside the forecastle was heavy, so he decided to risk a joke to lighten things up. He figured that the wretched Horowitz needed to understand that desertion is simply part of being a devoted sailor. They'd hardly left the plant when he tried to break the ice. With the utmost solemnity he said: So, it sounds like your old lady got tired of eating real Polish sausage and decided to go for the little Bedouin dates instead. Verrazano couldn't control himself and burst out laughing. Drake didn't react, so the Captain attacked the other man to show whose side he was on: I don't know what you're laughing at, fat ass. My slutty old lady says Italians got dicks the size of olives. The response was immediate, the same flurry of insults as every other day. Horowitz heard it as if from behind a waterfall. He had no desire to do anything, so he closed his eyes, hoping to sleep a little before they started dancing with the trash cans. Suspended in a drowsy darkness he heard very little after the Captain, believing him sound asleep, began to enjoy discussing the that amazing bit about the shit in the bed. In a serious voice he asked: How old do you think his little boy is? About three, the fat man answered. I wonder, said the old man, if he was standing there watching while her loverboy squeezed it out. Man, when he saw the size of that turd I bet he started clapping. Drake's eyes flew open, stricken with rage. He saw the Captain's shocked face for a moment before covering it with his hand and smashing the man's head against the window. Without loosening his grip on the driver, Horowitz grabbed the wheel with his right hand and pulled the truck off the highway. He yanked the hand brake, and when he felt the truck come to a complete stop, continued slamming the old man's head against the window until the glass was covered in blood. Verrazano stared at him in disbelief—truly surprised, perhaps, for the first time. This is a mutiny, Drake told him, his left hand still gripping the Captain's face, his right hand fishing in the bag for his rifle. Whose side are you on? The fat man didn't have to think twice: I'm for the people, he said. He took out the gun himself and pointed it at the Captain. Sorry, Cappy, but we've got a new set of rules.

They gagged him with duct tape, then bound his hands and feet with electrical cable. The old man offered no resistance. With obvious pleasure, Horowitz set him in the middle of the front seat and took over the wheel. They hadn't gone very far when Verrazano asked Horowitz what they were going to do with him. We're going to maroon him on an island. Then we'd better hurry, before the traffic picks up. They took the next left. Drake stopped the truck in the middle of the road. Between the two of them they carried the old man to the bushes. I'll let the police know you're here, Verrazano promised when he was sure that Horowitz was out of earshot. Before starting the truck again, Drake took a black flag from his duffel bag and tied it by two of its corners to the antenna on *Outrageous Fortune*.

What followed was barbarous depravity and cruelty: hot pursuit, ramming and boarding, assault, robbing and setting fire to a liquor store. Their broadsides against three parked minivans earned sufficient notoriety that for weeks afterward, housewives in the D.C. metro area would panic at the mere sound of a garbage truck rumbling by. Their spree lasted only a few, short hysterical hours. By noon they were already prisoners of their own catastrophe.

Heading north on a lightly traveled road with Verrazano at the wheel, they moored the ship on a backwater bend. Drake offered the only gambit he was willing to play: With what we've done today, you're gonna spend the rest of your life in jail, he said. He unfolded the chart and indicated a salt marsh in Chesapeake Bay. The only way to get there, he continued, is by following neighborhood streets. We can probably reach the place before they catch us. There's a big old marina, sticks way out into the sea. It's not used anymore. My dad took us there fishing sometimes. The fat man gathered what was left of his wits: I've got friends in prison. I'm sure I could make others once we're inside. Besides, I promised the Captain I was going to let someone know which island we stranded him on. Drake shrugged his shoulders. His companion added apologetically: There's nothing else we can do, Horowitz, my sympathy for your pain only goes so far. Then help me pilot the ship until we get there. I'd be delighted. Without saying another word, Horowitz left the forecastle and climbed the ladder to the poop deck. After bringing the ship about, Verrazano set a northeasterly course under full sail. For Drake the highway was the fresh, clean, wide-open sea. Tightly gripping the deck rail, he felt the sun on his face, the wind against his chest, and breathed the putrid smell of corruption rising from the bilge.

Filth

Long smooth slow swift soft cat
What score, whose choreography did you dance to
when they pulled the final curtain down?

Can such ponderous grace remain
here, all alone, on this 9 x 10 stage?

GREGORY CORSO

REFRIGERATION

After reaching a certain size, a secret generates a zone of silence around the one who carries it. Like a refrigerator, it has its own microclimate that people can poke their heads into but where no one else can remain. Every so often someone opened the door, the light would go on, and he would smile—his teeth like Tupperware containers—waiting patiently for the door to close again. What he wasn't sure about was whether he viewed reality as he did, like some prerecorded event, because he was leading a double life, or if his divergence from the world he inhabited since moving to the suburbs had led naturally to the strange condition of his feeling as though he were hiding in plain sight, the result of spending a certain amount of each day in secrecy. The question was: had his deficiencies led him to become a refrigerator or were they one more eventuality in his destiny as a refrigerator?

It came out during one of his first Thursday therapy sessions: The suburbs serve to protect the rest of the country from the peculiarities of the city, so those of us who live in them can't escape our own insulated condition; we're the martyrs of refrigeration, we cut a swath of mediocrity, and the daily commute from home to the city and back again allows the values of the rest of the country to remain exactly as they were when the Puritans stepped off the Mayflower to found the nation.

He didn't mention the part about feeling like a refrigerator; it was such a silly simile that he was a bit embarrassed about it, but sometimes he could feel the water pitchers, the vegetable crisper, and the slightly rancid cheese all sitting on his shelves. Nor did he mention it to Rob, his neighbor, the day when they discussed the problem of the suburbs. The weather was so hot that he felt like he was trapped inside a bubble from which it was impossible to make himself understood.

It went like this: he was crouched down planting *belenes* when he heard Rob say his name—or rather, that hollow, tortured sound he was now accustomed to identify with himself. He didn't raise his head because he didn't feel like it. Nor would he have done so at all but for the sweat dripping into his eyes; the moment after his neighbor insisted on tormenting the vowels in his name, he happened to have to wipe them with the back of one of his gardening gloves.

He lifted the hand he'd just used to wipe his eyes and said: Hey. Then he asked Rob how he was doing. Good, he answered him, what're you doing. I'm planting flowers. Each one waited for the other to say something else that had not yet occurred to their heat-addled brains. What kind are they, Rob finally asked. Impatiens, he replied, because that's what *belenes* are called in English. As it was obvious that his neighbor wasn't going to move from the spot until he got what he wanted, he asked what he could do for him. Can I borrow your mower? Help yourself. You know where it is. He turned his attention back to the soil, the flowers, and the slightly ridiculous trowel he was using to plant them.

He had always been a somewhat self-absorbed person, which is why he enjoyed the garden; during the time he spent working there he could forget about the ferocious competition at the office, the needs of his little girls, and the identity problems that so unsettled him, and which he didn't exactly understand. But since he had begun to lead a double life—maybe he had always done so, but without any palpable proof of its existence—he tried to practice as many solitary activities as possible: he spent more time swimming, tending his plants, watching TV.

What were you thinking so hard about, said Rob as he came back, pushing the lawnmower along the little tiled path that led from the garden to the street. I was thinking how the suburbs are the antidote we gringos whipped up for slavery. The other man thought about this for a moment then chose a noncommittal answer: You're not a gringo, he said. I am now, was the reply. Did you apply for citizenship? Yeah. And they gave it to you. Uh-huh. You swore on the flag and all that? Along with about four hundred Koreans. Congratulations. That's nice. I'll bring the mower back in a while. There's no hurry, I'm not cutting the grass today.

He waited until his neighbor had moved on before going into his house so that he wouldn't have to invite him in, and then he ran to the kitchen. The soft gust from the air-conditioning felt like a blessing. He was home alone—his wife and daughters had gone to a children's party and wouldn't return until the afternoon—so he slipped the cell phone out from his briefcase by the front door where it had been sitting since Friday evening when he got home from the Bank. He punched in the number he had decided not to store in its memory to avoid uncomfortable questions if his wife happened to find it. The answering machine took the call; as usual, she had her phone switched off whenever her husband was around. He didn't leave a message. He cracked open a beer and stood sipping it, staring out the window: the whole world outside wilting from the heat and him watching it like it was something on TV. He decided he couldn't stand another brush with reality, so he made himself a sandwich, then ate it, with a second beer, while watching baseball.

It wasn't until several weeks later that Rob reminded him about the suburbs and slavery. They were in the park, eating roast chicken at the picnic that the neighborhood school's parents association had organized to celebrate the start of the new school year. As always, the early September heat made it impossible to think clearly, and so killed any appetite for conversation he might otherwise have had. Each picnicker balanced a paper plate and plastic cup in one hand while trying to eat with the other.

What you said about slavery and the suburbs seems like a generalization to me, Rob said to him. At first he didn't understand what he was talking about; when his neighbor reminded him about the day he'd borrowed the lawnmower he tried to explain himself: It just seemed to me that white people have taken refuge in the outskirts of the cities to build themselves a world where there's no difference between themselves and the descendants of the people they kidnapped in Africa to work for them for free. In the suburbs, everything is sweet, middle class, and homogenous. Out here the original sin of slavery doesn't count; every little white house with its yard is an Ark of the Covenant. Rob put down his chicken leg on the paper plate and wiped his mouth on the sleeve of his T-shirt. He said: Although you're an American now, your grandparents weren't slave owners, mine weren't either; they were Quakers, from Pennsylvania; I moved to the suburbs because the public schools are good and I couldn't afford the tuition for a private school in the city. He shrugged his shoulders and thought that despite what everybody else thinks, gringos aren't so simple: they prefer never to commit themselves to any particular position. He told himself, as he did whenever he was having a hard time at the Bank: The essential thing for surviving in this country is to never say what you're thinking and then do whatever it is you feel like doing. He decided to act accordingly, so he held up his chicken breast and asked Rob what he thought about how the Orioles were doing. I'm not done

84

yet, his neighbor told him: The other thing is, you're not white. Yes, I'm white. No, you're not. And you aren't black. You're Latino. I'm Mexican. Not anymore. You're Latino now. Slavery is none of your business and you've got nothing to say about it.

I was born in Ciudad Satélite, a suburb of Mexico City, which doesn't in the least resemble what you folks call suburbia: for one thing, it's highly urbanized, and it actually has fewer trees than you find in the capital.

Although the continuity between Mexico City—*el Distrito Federal*—and Ciudad Satélite is never interrupted geographically, the two areas are completely different, because Satélite, like Washington, D.C., is a preplanned community, one designed with vaguely utopian ambitions, the product of a shady real estate deal.

Of course it is. Read your American history: having retired to his Virginia plantation, General Washington decided to resolve the dispute over where to build the capital, placing it next to the village of Georgetown, in Maryland, where his brother-in-law had a swamp for sale. He bought it for a song and sold it for a fortune to the federal government, which was then headed by his soul mate, President Jefferson. Then the two bastards, quite proud of themselves, their pockets stuffed with dollars, went to see John Adams inaugurated in the brand new city that, on top of it all, was named after the general. Well, that would even make them blush in Ciudad Satélite.

Anyway, I was born and raised in Ciudad Satélite. I went to school there, my girlfriends were from there; that's where I shopped at the supermarket and went to the movies.

Mexico City, which I didn't start to get to know until I went to university, always seemed wild, complicated, and snobbish to me, so I never suffered the excessive identification with my native soil that residents of the capital have. I visited Disneyland for the first time when I was six years old, and when my father's business was going well we took trips to Brownsville where we bought everything we had in our house. I never owned one single LP with songs in Spanish—in Ciudad Satélite listening to Mexican music was for servants—and I didn't know until I was twenty years old that there were movies in other languages than English; at the neighborhood video store the Mexican movies were catalogued in the Foreign Films section, alongside ones by Fellini or Kurosawa. I spent fifth grade as an exchange student at a school in New Orleans, and my MBA is recognized by Harvard but not by the Universidad Nacional in Mexico.

The United States was always familiar territory for me and I always thought it was a place very similar to Mexico, except better. Even so, when, as an adult, I moved to Atlanta for my brand new job at AT&T, I had the impression that I'd moved to China or Romania; that's how little I really understood my new environment. I never got used to life in Georgia. So, as soon as I could, I found a job at the World Bank and moved to Washington, D.C. I'd been told that the East Coast is a little more traditional and laid back, more like Mexico.

On my first weekend in D.C. I drove up to New York City to see an old high school friend who'd been living in the United States for seven or eight years. It didn't take more than one tequila for me to start telling him about my troubles. He sat there thinking about it for a minute, then said to me: What do you want me to tell you, 'mano? The USA is a country where soccer is a sport for little girls.

SALIVA

Out of all the connections he'd made at the World Bank, that city within a city, Malik was the closest thing he had to a friend. They'd shared a tiny cubicle when he started at the organization, and they developed an open, easygoing working relationship: they chatted at break time, strolled out together for a midmorning coffee, and shared part of the commute home to the suburbs on the Metro. Their conversations always had something of the comic routine in them, which the other employees in the Development Projects office found a little shocking.

The difference between his relationship with Malik and those he had with the rest of his acquaintances at the Bank lay exclusively in what they talked about. Malik had been born in Sri Lanka and raised in Boston. He was intelligent, cultured, progressive, and nobody among the few who knew him understood very well why he worked there. I've got four little savages to feed, was the most he offered as an explanation. The extent of his erudition regarding almost everything showed that he was essentially a reader: between the ruckus from his children and his wife's Hindu relatives, about whose endless visits he never stopped complaining, he must have spent his afternoons and evenings in some armchair in a little white house with a yard and garden, reading up on world culture.

The problem with gringos, Malik said to him one day, is that they don't know how to make conversation. They share their opinions when they feel authorized to do so, but they don't know how to sit down and talk about anything just to talk about it, without getting impatient. In Boston I used to live in the Hindu neighborhood, which is really something else, but since I came to the Washington suburbs, I'm like the deaf-mute of Sidon.

He recognized the Biblical sound of this deaf-mute reference, but he preferred not to ask: on a previous occasion when he'd shown his ignorance about Christian tradition, the Sri Lankan had worn himself out laughing at him. He waited until Malik went to the bathroom to make his ablutions—he was notoriously slow about it—to look up the reference on the Internet. He found it in a moment: it came from the Gospel of St. Mark.

Jesus departed the rich, illustrious, and orthodox region of Tyre, where he had been preaching in synagogues to his own class. He entered the poor Gentile region of the Decapolis, on the shores of the Sea of Galilee, where the people who had heard tell of him were more interested in his shamanic healing powers than in his reputation as a rabbi. During his first day staying in the Decapolis, a large crowd brought to him a man who was a deaf-mute. Resigned to his fame, Jesus drew apart a little from the spectators; he took the man by the shoulders and violently pushed him down onto his knees. He vigorously thrust a finger in the man's ear. With his free hand he forced open the deaf-mute's mouth, and in a single motion stretched out the man's tongue, letting fall on it a drop of his own saliva. He shouted at him *Ephphatha!*—which means *Be opened!*—and he tugged on the man's hands for him to rise. The man thanked him with perfect diction then asked what he could do to repay him. Jesus told him to keep his cure a secret. St. Mark doesn't say whether or not the man lived the rest of his life in the paradox of pretending to be a deaf-mute, although he relates that the man's companions didn't pay much attention to the Nazarene's orders.

When Malik returned from the bathroom, he was

waiting for him with a joke: *Ephphatha!*, he shouted when he saw him walk through the door, and in case his friend didn't remember the evangelist's exact text, he translated: Be opened! The Sri Lankan smiled. I've tried to, he added, but it always turns out worse: to be open you need someone who feels like listening, and gringos have enough problems being gringos without trying to listen to others.

A few days after talking with Malik about Jesus curing the man from Sidon, and his paradoxical destiny, the telephone on his desk rang. A secretary informed him that the Bank's Director of Communications wanted to speak with him, that he should come up to the third floor right away. It was then nine or ten o'clock in the morning and by lunch time he was already cleaning out his desk. He said goodbye to the Sri Lankan, who accompanied him to the elevator carrying a small box, and who did not once stop talking about the relationship between medieval mendicants and the modern day globalophobics who made their lives impossible with their demonstrations and protests.

The Communications Office was much more demanding than the catacombs of Development Projects, so much so that he was forced to alter his habits completely. He had no news about Malik for more than a year, until one day they happened to run into each other at the Middle Eastern kiosk in the Bank's food court. I haven't heard a thing about you, he said to his old office companion, a little bit embarrassed because it was obvious who had been the master and who the apprentice, and who should have been the one to call whom. I'm in the same place as always, in the asshole of the building, at the bottom of the ladder. And you? Moving right along: a few months after they called me up to Communications they promoted my boss to be regional director, so now I'm on the fourth floor, in an office with a window.

And you must be delighted. Delighted. In this company, the higher up you go the more sinister it gets, so I don't really envy you. That's why you're my hero. I don't want your admiration, I want money. That's what I need so I can quit this shitty job. As they walked to a table they caught up on the details of each other's lives. You're really skinny, the Sri Lankan told him when they were seated, I'm sure they've got you working morning, noon, and night. They do, he answered, but that's not why. Then it's from chasing skirts. More or less. *Ephphatha!*

Since I first accepted the job here and they put me into Development Projects with you, he told him, I was aware that a woman with whom I'd had a very intense relationship many years ago was living in D.C., married to a Bank employee. That was the only thing I knew, and it was only secondhand gossip because I hadn't been in touch with her since we split up. Then, one day, added the Sri Lankan as if to speed up the story, you ran into her buying milk in the shop on the first floor. No: the day after they promoted me to Communications she just showed up at my office out of nowhere and told me that I hadn't thanked her. When I recovered from my shock I asked her what for. She explained that she'd spoken about me to her husband and for that reason he'd had me promoted. She sat down in one of the chairs facing my desk and added: I told him that we'd been very close friends. And what are you doing here? I asked her. We've got tickets for the opera, but he's in a meeting. Shall I grab a couple of coffees so we can chat while we wait for him? Go get two coffees. Malik interrupted him, saying, with his eyebrows raised very high: She's your boss's wife? Yes. Now I don't know if I want to hear any more. You sound just like a gringo now. He half closed his eyes and conceded: *Ephphatha!* then continued: So, then you invited her to have lunch another day. No, I didn't see her again for two or three months: working in Development Projects leaves you no free time, but in Communications you basically have no personal life at all. So, then? So my boss got promoted to be director for the Pacific Basin and we threw a cocktail party in his honor, at Old Ebbit, a place he really likes because he used to work in the Treasury. On the way to the official appointment ceremony he stopped by my office and told me: I'll see you at the party, bring your wife along. Is yours coming? I asked him. He raised his hands as though praying to heaven and answered me: She's been driving me crazy for weeks, telling me how nice it was to see you, and how she's dying to meet your wife. By now Malik had finished his kebab, and said: So you hooked up with her right in front of everybody. No, it wasn't me: it just happened. We ended up chatting, and before I knew it we were sharing the same glass. Then she told me that she had a message she'd been keeping for me. What? I asked her. It's a message that can only be passed through the saliva, she answered. And she pushed you down on your knees, finished Malik, standing up from the table, and she opened your mouth, and she let fall a drop of her holy water on your tongue. That's a little much, but I guess you might put it that way. The Sri Lankan glanced at his watch and said: I don't have to leave yet, but the truth is, I don't want to hear any more.

THERAPY: GRINGOS

Australians were the dregs of British society; their country was a penal colony that became a nation. Besides there being something heroic in that assertion, there's also a real identification between the land and its occupiers: Australians are *from Australia*. We gringos can't even boast that much: we're the scum of the earth, the leftovers from all the other countries that came looking for a second chance.

It's nothing to laugh about. You were born here and they convinced you in school that it's the best country in the world, but sure enough, your father or your grandfather didn't think that way, did they, because they came from somewhere else.

Isn't that right?

This country is nameless, and we as its inhabitants have chosen, consciously and consistently, to have no patronymic: Salvadorans are Salvadoran, Chinese are Chinese, and the French are French. Gringos? We're African Americans, Mexican Americans, Native Americans, German Americans, Irish Americans. A woman at the Bank defines herself as a Bohemian American, and nobody remembers anymore, not even in the Czech Republic, that Bohemia was once a nation under Austro-Hungarian protection. We're neither an empire, nor a republic, nor a monarchy. We're nothing: it's every man for himself because no one wants to belong to the world of second chances. We're whatever slipped through the cracks of history: pure ambition without any ulterior commitments—a ragtag band of pirates. We're gringos and we urgently need some national therapy.

Don't laugh. Think of it as a business opportunity and you'll see that I'm right.

SAINT BARTHOLOMEW

Sown in dishonor, it is raised in glory.

I CORINTHIANS 15:43

He told her that he'd gone to church one day and that the Polish baritone had just disappeared, his wife and all their children too: now they hadn't been to Mass in three weeks.

He said it apropos of nothing, simply to fill up a moment of silence, perfectly aware of the fact that this was the first she was hearing about the singer. It was an incidental sort of anecdote, and he probably thought to bring it up just for a laugh, but it pulsed with something sadder and less explicable: talking on cell phones made him tense because—he thought—it conjures up a frustrating and illusory sense of nearness; information is accelerated but nothing is communicated, at least not in the strict sense of the word. No matter how much you want it to, an empty, disembodied voice does not represent an act of communion. He felt that their calls were like some exam that he had to pass, or simply survive.

Sometimes they talked for a specific reason—to agree on a cover story, to avoid some careless slip—but most of the time they called each other just to call. It was a ritual, an act of acquired, gratuitous risk, something that had begun one day and quickly acquired a life of its own: at one time it would simply have felt right now and then to call, but now it was a ritual, something they'd come to expect. Sometimes it was a good call, sometimes not, but it formed a strand in a vast web of expectations and anxieties to which they were now well accustomed. Perhaps those ten minutes plundered from the wasteland of the day helped them—like going to church—to show each other that they weren't gringos, not yet, not completely.

They'd been chatting about how the big, full congregations seen at the Spanish Masses were so moving: the preposterously criminal in the same throng as the faithful, he said. Then he explained how, in spite of that, he preferred the cosmopolitan coldness of the nine o'clock Mass—in English: with Filipinos, Lebanese, Irish, Koreans, Italians—because, for one, it was progressive and distinguished; then, for another, it provided him with the opportunity to witness the weekly skirmish in the Polish baritone's ongoing battle.

Either the singer and his wife were the last gringos attentive to the Vatican's stance on reproduction or they had learned from the Irish that all triumphs are, in the end, statistical; the Protestants would have to be beaten through sheer numbers. At the Hispanic Mass, their seven unwashed children wouldn't have seemed such a terrible disaster, but compared to a typical English-speaking family—a few adults and a single child—they were absolutely scandalous. Seven? she asked him, thinking he must be exaggerating. Seven, he answered, five boys and two girls.

Before the watchful eyes of the parish, the clan had grown to an uncontrollable size, and the children's disarray had naturally increased in direct proportion to their quantity: the younger ones' clothing had already been worn threadbare by their older siblings, who were also better fed. The mother, a beanpole of suspiciously Calvinistic propriety and severity when times were good, had gone flabby, swollen, and purple beneath some dresses that were, by now, quite snug. The baritone was still red-faced and robust but his beard was badly trimmed and his tennis shoes were a disgrace; the alterations stitched into the underarms of his shirts gave notice of a sudden, unhealthy increase in weight. They would have been a normal enough family in the 1970s, a time when modesty was not yet considered a defect, but among the perfectly trimmed and outfitted congregation at nine o'clock Mass they seemed more like a band of castaways.

There was a time—by now a part of the parish mythology—when the baritone attended Mass from his place on the musicians' risers, to the right of the altar, his back to the organist, lavishly pouring out his implacable voice alongside a Ugandan woman draped in curtain-like dresses. His proliferating offspring, however, obliged him to move down to mingle with the multitude: his wife found it impossible to maintain order among the children herself. There were three or four unbearable Masses before the singer decided to leave stardom behind, urged forward—it was murmured—by the priest, who could no longer continue casting the pearls of his religious office before a herd of swine being distracted by a bunch of little brats fighting over some completely worn-out toy.

The opening section of the first Mass that the baritone spent back on terra firma felt something like a surrender: likely prompted by resentment, he didn't allow himself to be tempted by the music, and the truth is that he was missed: his singing talent was far too good for a church like that. His children still behaved quite badly, only tempered now by a certain shyness; it seemed that the fat man, who did nothing to control them, only barely commanded their respect. The Ugandan woman sang alone up to the Acclamation, when the Pole couldn't stand it any longer and quietly, humbly joined in singing with the rest of the faceless congregation.

To hear his voice again amid the Hosannas was like a sooth-ing balm: in the end, the main reason for attending Mass during eras when faith seems to be on the wane is to dem-onstrate that, regardless of how prodigal he has been, the son can always return home; that one is permitted to follow a little in the footsteps of his parents and grandparents.

So, are you taking the girls? she interrupted him. He'd been so focused on sustaining the flow of his narrative that he didn't see her curveball coming. Where? To church. Of course, he said, it's good for them, a civilizing influence: the Mass is the story that explains all the other stories, even if I don't believe in it. I do. I'm jealous. And does she go? Who? Your wife. He hesitated a bit before answering. Sometimes. Isn't she Lutheran? Yes, and that's why.

The duet remained stable for a few more Masses: the Ugandan woman on the riser—a goddess in drapery—and the Pole in the pews below, an exiled Romeo. But nothing lasts forever, he said; bound by duty, the Ugandan woman heeded her community's call, becoming the regular soloist in the choir at the twelve o'clock Mass with its congregation composed of recently arrived African immigrants.

Then the war began. Probably angry because the priest, until he found a different singer, preferred to conduct the ceremony solely with organ music, the baritone began to use his whole voice—trained in who knows what conserva-tory to fill theaters of Soviet dimensions—with the goal of blowing away the other worshipers who, sparse and timid, tried to follow the organist in their blue psalm books. On the two Sundays that it took the priest to place a substitute on the riser, the Pole launched the same string of provoca-tions. He opened by intoning the antiphon at a barbarous volume that he only increased following the Gloria. By the offertory he had become the lord of all the air in the church, such that he raised or lowered his tone just enough to throw the priest off course—even with a microphone clipped to his cassock, the priest had a very hard time competing with him.

When the moment arrived to exchange the sign of peace, the priest and the congregation had already surrendered, so that the last man standing was the organist, who was also the toughest nut to crack. The baritone's strategy, nevertheless, was infallible. He faithfully followed the keyboard's tempo up to the point when he felt that he could flatten it, then unleashed the full power of his voice box, and once he had the melody in his pocket, he slowed or accelerated the time at will. The organist's bald head glowed red with fury when he discovered—thanks to a slight delay on the parts of the other faithful worshippers—that he had lost control of the music. So that the ceremony wouldn't lose its solemnity, he had no other remedy but to follow the enemy.

This was the fat man's moment of glory. Although he and his brood always occupied the front pew on the right-hand side of the nave, they waited until the paterfamilias had won his duel to the death with the organist to stand up and receive Communion. Their approach to the chalice practically stopped the show. The baritone walked slowly behind his wife, bearing the whole rite in his throat, luminous from the effort, and surrounded by his entire retinue of seven children. When his turn came, he cut off his singing, regardless of their place in the psalm, and bowed his head with a sincerely peaceful gesture that he maintained until finishing his prayers. That, in some way, revealed the irreproachably Catholic quality of his mettle: his body, liberated in full triumph over the banality of its earthly battles, was a perfect lesson on the redemptive power of a god supposedly incarnate in human flesh.

When he finished praying, he rose to his feet like a triumphant bullfighter and, before sitting down, gave the congregation a happy look—he supposed they were on his side. The organist received a malevolent smile; although he had already recovered his preeminent position, for the time being, he knew that he'd lost his weekly opportunity to show off his middling flights of virtuosity.

The war of the Polish baritone, he said to her, as if reforming his own front line in preparation for the final assault of the enemy that was the same senseless story he was telling, is the ritual within the ritual found within the walls of Christ the King church. With a certain relief, he heard what sounded like a nasal tone of approval, although it might have just been interference: he usually phoned her from the Starbucks on H Street, two or three blocks from the Bank, to avoid the discomfort of watching her husband walk past while he was trying so hard to make her laugh.

The priest tried various recourses, each time with worse results. He hired a tall old Puritan woman, clean and ugly, hoping that her persistent, piercing high notes would drill through the baritone's bulk. She was steamrolled during the Kyrie. This woman returned the following Sunday, better armed: the sacristan had set up a microphone for her on the podium, one even better than the priest's own. When the poor woman began singing the penitential rite, the Pole raised his eyebrows then pulverized her without removing his hands from his pants pockets. The organist's bald head turned purple as an archbishop's mantle. After the Puritan woman's failure there was a very young Jamaican man whose angelic flight through the world was inevitably brought to ground by a flailing plunge from the ethereal heights of the Responsorial Psalm. Then came, in succession, a rosy giant of a man, pink as a pig; the rabid Dominican woman who directed the choir for the Mass in Spanish; and three unflappable Filipino *señoras*, fearless because they knew no one had any idea what they were singing. Three risers had to be stacked up for them to reach the microphone. It was no use. The Pole continued tyrannizing the Mass with his lungs of steel. Surrounded by his swarming progeny during the slow, majestic procession toward the altar and host, he was the full, vigorous embodiment of Slavic tenacity, destroying tempos and pushing notes to the breaking point.

Then he disappeared. It wasn't until he said this to her that he really and with clarity saw that he was telling a story with no ending. How? she asked, sounding very intrigued. For a moment this gave him the hope that something real was flowing along those microwaves, same as when they were guided only by the inscrutable, magnetic wisdom of the flesh, with nothing else in between them.

He disappeared, he said, that's all, nothing else. And? Well, we ended up stuck with the Filipino ladies—they're frightful. It can't be. The truth, he answered, is that I really miss him, so much that I went looking for him at Our Lady Queen of Poland. It's pretty close by. I went to all three morning Masses but there was no sign of him. He disappeared. Maybe he went on vacation, she said. Or he defected to Poland, he responded. Her laughter on the other end of the line made him feel that, in spite of everything, he might be able to save himself.

THERAPY: DUPLICITY

I have the strange and terrible habit of confessing offenses I haven't committed.

One day, for example, in my hour of deepest sincerity, beweeping our own incarnation of mankind's fall from grace, I told her that she had not been my only extramarital affair, that I'd had two other lovers. The number I decided on is of particular interest, because I'd never really had any.

But it would be more interesting still to know why I bother doing this. The fact is that, while confessing to these affairs, I was convinced about the veracity of the events in question. But they made no sense: we're both adults and we've been around the block enough times to be freely admitted to the ranks of the "experienced." My bragging, therefore, was unnecessary. But that's what I said to her and now I don't know how to take it back, because my fictional jadedness isn't consistent with my fears of our being found out.

It's something I've done ever since I was a kid: I pretend to have a secret life, all to myself. Well, now I've got it, all right, and nobody else can get in. I'm like the blind man in the Bible: although his sight was restored, he had to pretend that he couldn't see anything because Jesus Christ himself ordered it.

No, I don't even know if what I'm saying here is the truth.

FATHER

It was by no means a noteworthy event, but it came back to him whenever he allowed himself enough perspective to consider the more practical than admirable scale of values according to which he had always operated, and that had lately, for lack of opportunity, fallen into disuse. During a New Year's Eve celebration he'd gone out to the garden to have a smoke. He was with his wife and little girls at his father-in-law's house in Raleigh—a minor, tepid, nondescript city composed almost entirely of suburbs. A fine frozen rain was falling, which in the southern United States can begin at the end of November and not let up until March or April, without ever turning to snow. He had not yet removed his cigarette lighter from his jacket pocket when he spotted an opossum on the garden fence, just above eye level. It was very young, soaking wet, watching him with a hard, unsettling stare.

As was generally the case, the opossum story came back to him during a peaceful interval: she'd accompanied her husband on a business trip to Hong Kong, a trip he had helped to organize, so his days at the office crawled lazily by, without his boss's demands for action or his boss's wife's need for attention. During that time he checked his e-mail constantly because he knew that a message from her might arrive at any moment. He responded with long, intense letters that always made him feel less lonely while he wrote them, but which ended up being counterproductive. Perhaps because of its visual and sonic potency, the Web made him suppose that he had the world in the palm of his hand, and he was always somewhat disappointed to discover it was not so: despite his being able to read the news from Mexico with the intensity of someone who could still be directly affected by it, she was, in reality, in a Saigon cybercafé, and he was stuck inside the white monster of the World Bank—an air-conditioned Moby Dick—and what lay outside was the District of Columbia.

The story probably wouldn't have significance for anyone else, even if they knew its secret. There was no way to know, really: he'd told it to his father one day, many months after it had happened to him. He did so in response to a message in which his father had reported that he'd taken his other grandchildren to the zoo in Chapultepec Park, where he'd noted an air of unbearable servitude in the animals' eyes. As he supposed, the story of the opossum didn't arouse any reaction: the next message from his father, which arrived almost a week later, was short on animal lore. Perhaps—it had occurred to him while expounding on details completely inappropriate in a letter to the world's busiest man—he was telling all this to his father as a cry for help: he would have loved to sit down and have a drink with him and ask if he'd ever been in the same situation, but there was an insurmountable protocol separating them, according to whose rules male relatives may not share any information about their emotional lives.

It's not really unusual to step outside at night and see one of those animals—he wrote his father—but at the same time it's not so common as to be unworthy of celebration. During the warm seasons of the year, opossums live near some creek or gully; during the cold months, they occupy the blind spaces of the neighborhoods. They're the cats of the cold, the digestive system of suburbia when it's freezing out. Big and clumsy, they do their duty with the furtive dignity of the very ugly: they're the phantoms of an ecosystem sustained by trash cans, the filth in an impeccable white world which is played out in little houses, each with its own garden, that go on and on, perfect and identical, into infinity.

He didn't want to miss the privilege of having a smoke while contemplating such a strange animal, so he went ahead and lit his cigarette as cautiously as he could. He stood motionless, at a distance, smoking, his gaze fixed on the creature, which never took its eyes off him. When he had only a couple of drags left he decided to move closer: that it might get startled and run away was no longer so important: the cold rain was going to force him back inside the house soon anyway. Cautious as ever, he took a few steps; the opossum remained motionless. It was so young that perhaps it had not yet learned that fear is the basis of experience. He exhaled a final puff of smoke, tucked the cigarette between his thumb and index finger then flicked it away, far from the animal, which barely took its eyes off him long enough to see the burning tip of the butt fly through the air.

Until getting closer, he hadn't realized that the opossum was barely larger than a rat. He extended his hand, with the palm outstretched, as if it were a puppy. The animal uncurled, shook itself off, and waddled along to the other end of the fence, where it settled down again without once looking away. By now he was trembling from the cold, so he went back into the house.

Inside he found all the nervous preparations for dinner underway. His wife told him to set the table, his regular chore at family celebrations: Latin Creole and Catholic, he had, in the family's Lutheran landscape, an undisputed touch for livening up the whole presentation; there's nobody like him when it comes to arranging the instruments of our prosperity, his father-in-law liked to say, with the slightly worried look of those patriarchs whose daughters have moved beyond their reach. The first time he'd set the table, his father-in-law's wife had stared suspiciously at the splendors of her own board, but over time she'd learned to enjoy the fleeting excess. Shortly after a spring vacation they'd spent in Raleigh, it was her turn to host a meeting of her book club. After setting the table in her own gringo fashion it seemed like a paltry offering, so she redid it, imitating his Creole arrangement: no concealed weapons, everything in sight: the oil, vinegar, salt, pepper, and sauces, the dishes overflowing, the sliced bread laid in its basket, the bottles like gun barrels—one for every three guests—aimed straight up at the ceiling and heaven beyond, and the menacing sugary desserts laid out on the sideboard. Perhaps it was a coincidence, but this dinner turned out to be the most successful one so far. How exciting, said a neighbor, feeling caught between the abundance and her own embarrassment.

When he wrote to his father, he was aware that what he'd be looking for in his son's messages were stories about the girls—he adored them because they were *gringas* but also never stopped worrying that they were too gringo. He knew that his father printed out his messages and took them home to read to his mother, and that she fantasized for days over the paragraphs about how her granddaughters were growing. For this reason he took special care to mention how the older girl, who was about to turn five years old that New Year's, helped him as best she could with the unbreakable table utensils. The younger girl was still just a baby, and really didn't do much of anything, so at the end he added a paragraph about an imaginary cough that she'd just gotten over.

Their New Year's Eve celebration went on as usual, as he related in the e-mail: they ate dinner, and after putting the little girls to bed, turned on the television and sat down together to watch the countdown to midnight. As the year's-end special didn't look very promising, they made a strong pot of coffee to help them stay awake and keep the party going for three more hours. He took the last of his coffee outside with him when he went to have another smoke. The opossum was still there, trembling from cold and fear.

When he went back inside he mentioned his discovery. The first time he hadn't said anything, but this second encounter now struck him as odd. With his in-laws he didn't take the same perverse pleasure in reflecting on recycling and the filth in the suburban ecosystems as he did several months later in his e-mail to his father: in English, in the provinces, musing without specific meaning sounded like intellectualizing, suspiciously lacking in sincerity and simplicity. He said that there was an opossum crawling on the fence, that it was very young, that it had probably come down from a tree and couldn't get back up to safety in the branches. Hardly looking away from the screen, his in-laws mentioned that there was plenty of wildlife in the neighborhood thanks to the creek nearby. The presence of opossums was a good sign because they ate snakes. His wife appeared a bit more interested: she was moved by the idea that it was a young animal. Are we going to help it get down? she asked him, but he had already surrendered to the spell of the TV and didn't feel like getting wet again. It's just got to get up the nerve to jump down to the grass, that's all, he said. His father-in-law observed that, no matter what, it would be neither safe nor hygienic to try to trap it, not just like that, without any preparations. If it was still there in the morning, they would go outside with the necessary equipment to help it.

That exchange, on the other hand, he chose not to share

with his father because it wasn't his habit to complain. He kept writing, explaining how, with just twenty minutes remaining until midnight, he got up for the third time. He knew that he wasn't going to have another smoke until just before going to bed because of what was coming up—they would wait for the clock on TV to strike midnight, followed by a very awkward round of embraces, then share a bottle of champagne so slowly that the glasses got warm while watching the stars on this or that TV special.

As he came back into the room, his wife asked him if the opossum was still stuck on the fence. He said yes. Partly out of genuine curiosity—all recurrent history is always noteworthy—partly because the slow, pleasant moments of letting their meal settle had passed, and partly because the mounting series of commercials at midnight, one after another, made the programming unbearable, the problem now received the whole family's attention. His wife thought that all the fireworks at midnight were going to give the poor animal a fatal heart attack, and that was reason enough to spur them into action. His father-in-law accompanied him back outside and confirmed that the opossum was still trapped by the height of the fence. He disappeared a moment in the direction of the toolshed and returned carrying a board. He'd put a cap on his head and had some yellow, wool-lined, waterproof overalls covering his clothes. It's my winter gear, he said, leaning the board up against the wall so he could zip himself up to the neck and put on his gloves. He had another pair in the back pocket of his overalls. He held them out to his son-in-law in case he needed help. Between the two of them they carried the board and propped it up to make a ramp from the top of the fence down to the grass. That's it, said his father-in-law with satisfaction, it can get down by itself, nobody needs to touch it.

They got back in the house with more than enough time to drink their toast and share that hug.

He smoked his last cigarette a little before one o'clock in the morning. The opossum had disappeared, so he removed the board and put it back in the toolshed. Once in bed, his wife looked up for a moment from the pages of the enormous biography of John Adams she was reading and asked him about the animal. He was touched that she thought to ask about the little drama in which he'd played the starring role. It crossed the bridge we set up for it, he responded, and it's free. She smiled and kissed him. See, you were a hero. She turned back to her book. He'd started to concentrate on the case study about Ecuadoran fishing disputes that he'd brought to read when his wife looked up again. Poor animal, she said, it must be thinking that it made such a great escape.

THERAPY: THERAPY

Meanness and selfishness are the only values that count in a society that prides itself on being composed of immigrants. That's why, sooner or later, all of us gringos end up going to therapy. In a world like this one, the only way to get someone to listen to you is by paying them to do it.

WHITE

> Eyes without feeling, feeling without sight.
> Ears without hands or eyes.

> *Hamlet*: Act III; Scene 4

During Major League postseason playoffs, time all across the country comes to a halt when a game starts. The one that evening wound up in a tie at the top of the ninth inning, and ended up going on until well after midnight. The twelfth inning was so tense that he didn't even take a sip of the gin and tonic he'd mixed himself to drink while he watched. When the game ended, he added some fresh ice and stayed up a little while longer, enjoying the singular freedom that comes from being awake in a house where everyone else is asleep. There was nothing else worth watching on TV, so he switched off the set and reached for the bookshelf to pick up the video camera he'd bought last winter.

He turned it on, rewound the tape a little, and pressed the play button. On the plasma screen a pure white color appeared, then a blue strip in the upper part of the frame. The vibration of the strip made it clear that the camera was moving, although the big white patch remained static. After a few seconds some vertical bars that he was slow to recognize as trees moved in and out of the frame. At last his own face appeared, talking about the snow and the cold. It was part of a documentary that the girls had filmed on a visit downtown during the record snowfall, which was the very reason for their buying the camera.

Those were unusual, noteworthy days: his wife was out

of town, gone to be with her mother in Philadelphia where the latter was recovering from an operation. He was left to contend with their two young daughters and the heavy weather alone.

The snow began falling around noon on a Tuesday already filled with anticipation. He was seated at his desk editing a report, blinds drawn to block the light reflecting off the computer screen, when his boss appeared: It's already started snowing, he told him, and it's heavy. I'm gonna stay late because I've got a conference call with the consultants in San Francisco, but I can walk home if they close the Metro. You should head home now. You can send me the report by e-mail.

When he found himself alone in his office he opened the blinds wide. What he liked about the beginning of a snowstorm was the fact that the enormous agitation produced by people getting their errands done before all the businesses closed kept the streets completely full. The panorama offered a fleeting illusion: the sky above dissolving into a ferocious whiteness that threatened all the colors of life down below. Getting up, he made sure that his boss had gone back into his office then discreetly closed the door to his own. He called her number on his cell phone; she was just leaving a benefit luncheon nearby. He looked at his watch: it was a few minutes after one o'clock. They arranged to see each other, even though it was just for a short while before he headed back to the suburbs. Then he called his house and told the Argentine woman who looked after the children that he had to attend a business meeting, but that he would be home early.

It snowed heavily without stopping all through the night—all of Wednesday, and half of Thursday. The snow-flakes were the size of walnuts, at times. The temperature

111

stayed well below freezing, so that the snow piled up steadily without slowing down.

What was at first celebrated as a blessing—in Washington, D.C., schools, banks, and the federal government all shut down at the slightest threat of inclement weather—became, after the first twelve hours, a cause for concern: the first morning he had to climb out of the house through the windows to shovel away the snow that didn't stop falling, and then keep clearing it away every little while to keep open their only exit. He dug an exhausting system of tunnels out from the front door so that they could reach the trash cans—the kitchen door remained blocked—and to get to the toolshed, where he kept the sleds and other snow toys. The car, which they never parked in the garage, was completely buried, and the whole street was a snowdrift that reached up to his chest and was well over his older daughter's head.

On Wednesday, starting early in the morning, they had a fantastic time, sledding down the hills in the park. The forced break brought on by the snow put the whole neighborhood into a mood unlike any he'd seen before. All his neighbors gathered on the slopes, in such a way that the upper part of the hill looked like a beach: dozens of adults and their dogs watching children sliding down deep into a white sea. In the afternoon, back at the house, they raised an igloo and built a giant snowman, then glutted themselves on hot chocolate. After putting the girls to bed he spoke on the phone with his wife: he was getting worried that the county workers had not yet begun plowing the streets.

On Thursday they took things easier: they watched cartoons all morning before going out to play. Then they opened up the igloo, whose doorway had become buried during the night. They tracked, without much luck, the paw prints of

112

some hungry raccoon that had been foraging in the yard for food. After lunch they noticed that it had stopped snowing and the sun was just peeking through, so they went to go sledding again. Lacking the energy of the day before, they soon returned to the house, where they watched cartoons the rest of the afternoon. The girls were delighted to have sausages for dinner a second time, but he wasn't so thrilled: he was getting fed up with his own lousy cooking. They didn't hear the roar of a snowplow that day either.

On Friday he spent the morning digging out the car, possessed by the hope that they would soon be clearing the street. In the afternoon they dragged the sleds to the hill, but after sliding down the first time they noticed how difficult it was to climb back up because the snow had turned to a sheet of ice. They made snow angels on the park's basketball court, then almost got hypothermia pretending to be Eskimos living in the igloo. They watched all the cartoons on TV. For dinner, he thawed out some hamburgers.

They were out of juice, but still had enough things for breakfast, lunch, and dinner through Sunday. If the snowplow didn't come by then to clear their street, on Monday he and the two girls were going to have to make a big supermarket run on the bus. The very thought of such a trip seemed nightmarish: the emergency route used by public transit was four blocks away, a distance he would not normally have minded walking, but the idea of hauling the shopping bags through such deep snow struck him as actually frightening.

Sunday morning was, frankly, abysmal. After lunch—he was washing the dishes from their lunch of tuna and saltines—his older daughter realized that they had not taken any pictures of the igloo to show their mother, so they got out the camera only to discover that it had no film. Let's go

113

buy some, he told them, with the joy of one surprised to find himself set free. He dressed them as if they were going on an expedition to the North Pole and they walked to the Metro station; even though it was a little bit farther than the bus stop, it took them right to the shopping mall.

Life there seemed to be following its normal routine. They spent the afternoon buying snacks, thankful for the novelty of the scene. At some point they sat down to have an ice cream and he realized that he had not seen a black person since Tuesday, nor any Arabs, Hindus, Asians, or Mexicans: only his own neighbors, whiter than ever for the wintertime lack of sunshine. The folksy look of the gangbangers at the next table sporting their NFL jerseys and clownish sneakers was comforting to him. As the afternoon wore on, the girls proposed getting a video camera to tape a report. So they went to buy it. Tomorrow, he told them as he was paying, we're going skating at the rink, if school's still out, and we'll do our shooting then.

He didn't like watching himself on the screen—his face looked wider and flatter than it did in the mirror and he couldn't even recognize his profile—so he rewound the tape until he found a part that he had shot himself. He located it right away and then kept rewinding. He saw the girls walking backward into the door of the skating rink at the sculpture garden, the confusion of the people skating back-ward and the girls among them, holding hands, cracking up laughing and picking themselves up from the ice every now and then. He saw them taking off their skates and putting on their sneakers in reverse order, leaving backward through the entry and saying hello to the camera. Then followed random sequences of the white capital.

The shots stopped their dizzying advance at an unusual moment that he had completely forgotten: in the middle of one frame there was a pickup truck perched whimsically on a snowdrift about three feet tall, high enough so that the truck wouldn't have had enough traction to drive over it. He took his finger off the rewind button and listened to his own voice discussing with the girls the impossibility of what they were seeing. He heard himself say that it was so strange it seemed as if the truck had been lowered from a helicopter.

By that time he had spent several days meditating on the spectacle of the snow and the purification ritual it performs in a society that believes itself born to rule by virtue of race. With the snow just starting to fall, he had glimpsed in the distance, from a room on the fifth floor of the Washington Hotel, the snowy landscape of Pennsylvania Avenue, ostentatiously white by nature: the White House and the Treasury building in the foreground, the narrow, foreshortened canyon between the museums along the Mall, Congress at the far end—all marble. Seen from above, it had occurred to him, the city had the quality of a poisoned dessert. What? she asked—they were leaning on the inside sill of the closed window, their hips, shoulders, arms touching, nothing in between. He said that for the rest of the East Coast it was just a big blizzard, but in the capital it was Mother Nature's affirmation of Manifest Destiny. She laughed and asked him when he'd stopped being pro-Yankee. Since you started working at the World Bank? Since I became a gringo, he replied. She added that he was imagining things. Why had he bothered to become a citizen if he was just going to complain about it? The only thing wrong with you, she concluded, is that you work too much. Just like my husband. Then she sent him home: You've got to go; the girls will start to worry.

Now down in the Metro, nearly deserted, he found a little folded paper inside his eyeglass case. It was a note written on a tiny white circular sheet, like a communion host, perhaps slightly larger. He unfolded it, knowing that it was a message from her: she always left him notes written on her own delicate stationery. He read the words, printed in a Catholic schoolgirl's writing: Tonight I'll step out on the balcony and open my mouth, each snowflake a drop of your semen. He considered it for a moment, folded it back up and ate it: he usually disposed of the evidence immediately, even when, as in the subway car, there was no trash can.

By five o'clock in the afternoon it was completely dark and he was already back home—his house felt increasingly like a shirt that was out of fashion. Between the girls' excitement and the TV news announcement that buses throughout the county would stop running at nine o'clock, the Argentine babysitter was hysterical. He sent her home with a generous tip.

He played the video to see if he could recognize in the shots taken at the skating rink the men they would later identify as the owners of the pickup stuck on the snowdrift. The screen was too small and the throng of skaters too thick for him to spot them. The one thing he was sure of was that they had filmed the moment when they freed the truck from the pile of snow, so he pressed the fast forward button.

The owners of the truck had caught their attention before they even knew who they were. At the shopping mall they would have passed by unnoticed, but at the skating rink filled with white people coursing over the white ice among the white monuments, they stood out scandalously. They were four heavyset guys who looked very much alike and called each other *güey*—"dude"—something only a Mexican would say.

When the girls got tired, long before the two-hour skate rental was up, actually a little too quickly, considering the long ride on public transit from the suburbs, he took them to have some hot chocolate at the cafeteria across from the skating rink. They waited until they warmed up again before heading back to the Metro. On their way there, they saw the fat guys again, walking along like four giant penguins in their high-visibility jackets.

In a low voice he mentioned to his older daughter how clownish the four men looked. It was thanks to people like that, she told him, that kids at school gave her a hard time for being a Mexican's daughter. The fat men kept walking until the next block where they stopped in front of the pickup truck. One of them took the keys out of his pocket with boyish pride while the others joked around. It can't be, he said to his daughter: my Mexican brothers are the owners. God only knows how they got it up on that snowbank, but there's no way they can get it down and drive it out of there. His youngest daughter had gotten a little bit ahead of them; he shouted her name so she would stop: he wanted to enjoy the spectacle of the fat guys watching the traction fail on their cowboy pickup.

He pulled out the video camera and shot the scene, which he now watched again with disbelief: without any of them having to give orders, the four tubby figures soon stopped fooling around and separated; each took up a position at a corner of the pickup. The one with the keys in his hand—who had stayed in front, on the driver's side—counted to three and they began to rock up and down in the snow, first raising the truck's front bumper for a brief instant, then the rear: after each bounce, they whistled to signal the next movement. In less than ten seconds—he counted them as he watched the video—the truck had been freed from the snowbank and was back on the pavement. The four Mexicans took off their jackets and got into the cab, where the

117

driver had already been running the heater. It was obvious that, once, inside the truck, they went off having just as much fun as they'd been having outside: they were what they were.

In that moment the image went all shaky for a few seconds before he himself appeared in the frame. It seemed that his daughter had asked him for the camera, or that he had handed it to her, because he could see himself searching through his wallet for their Metro tickets. When he looked back at the camera, his face wore a bitter expression; he said that he couldn't stop thinking about his Odyssey, stuck fast in the pristine suburban snow.

He took a swallow of his gin and tonic, thinking that if they were already onto the third game of the World Series, it was just a question of weeks, a month and a half at the most, before it started snowing again. He watched himself with disgust, gesturing within the plasma screen, and said: *Now cracks a noble heart. Good night, sweet prince.* He shut off the camera.

Grand Finales

THE EXTINCTION OF DALMATIAN

Fortune came to Tuone Udina on his rock, almost twenty years after he lost his hearing. Gnarled and dry, somewhere between green and gray, every afternoon while the good weather lasted he sat on a crest of rock that the biting iron air off the Adriatic Sea had stripped bare of life.

Night was settling in with imperial majesty when a man appeared, coming toward him, dressed with ridiculous formality for the rather rugged world of the island of Veglia. Barely protected by the jacket and vest of his tight, brown, woolen suit, it was obvious that he was freezing cold, but he gestured calmly and courteously, as if speaking to someone else. Udina didn't have much basis for comparison, but the difference between his visitor's almost excessively polite gestures and the rough manners of the man whose sheep he cared for was, at the very least, disquieting.

The stranger stopped and stood between Tuone and the valley, his back to the sea, looking up at the peak of the hill whose shoulders ran through the rock. Safe from the world in his deafness, the shepherd stared fixedly for a time at the man who moved his arms like a young woman while he talked: his marquesa's fingers—fat, clean, childlike—pointing now and then toward one place or another, his eyebrows moving up and down precisely in time with the long, slow rhythm of the mustache bristling above his lips; every so often he pushed his eyeglasses up against the bridge of his nose. And then he'd stopped moving, was looking down; rubbing the sole of his small, finely tooled leather boot against the grass as if he'd stepped in some shit and his life depended on his scraping it off. Then he combed his mustache with the tips of his fingers, scratched his perfectly

121

trimmed beard, or ran his tiny infantile index finger between his neck and the celluloid collar fastening his shirt.

Udina had never been able to guess the age of city people, for which reason he never knew who was respectable and who owed *him* respect; for that reason, and because he didn't like the disconcerting looks they gave him while he talked, he'd stopped taking the ferry that carried the villagers to the better-stocked island of Rijeka. On Veglia, with patience and without opening his mouth, he could obtain the frugal sustenance a shepherd requires. Now he paid attention because his visitor was sure to be wealthy. Hands folded in his lap, nodding his head every so often, he kept on looking at the man as if he could really hear him. Conscious of the fact that his naked, purple, toothless gums looked revolting, he didn't smile even once. After a while, however, he was distracted by a glimmer from out at sea, the last rays of sunlight glinting off the smokestack of the weekly steamer that connected Rijeka with the mainland port of Dubrovnik.

Tuone did not find his hermit's life disagreeable: in fact, he considered himself lucky for having gained the protection of a Croatian landlord during the atrocious weeks of the War of the Brothers. No one among his family or friends in the town had survived the marauding bands of soldiers who purged the island of Dalmatians when the rumor spread that the government in Vienna was conspiring with them. Losing his hearing was the small price he paid for the privilege of being able to go on watching the glorious evening sky over the Illyrian islands: he wasn't in the village during the extermination campaigns, but a sheep fell into one of the mines loaded with gunpowder that the partisans had buried in the fields atop the cliff. He was approaching to rescue it when it set off the detonator.

Coming to his senses a short while later—the sun had not yet reached the zenith—he checked to see if he was missing any body parts. He stood up and moved his arms and legs to make sure they obeyed him. He wiped the mud from his face and stood there a moment staring at the blast crater. Then he rounded up the sheep that had run off. The whistling sound that held on like the last lone dweller inside the passageways in his head gradually faded away to silence.

When he returned to the village many years later—the heir to the farm convinced him that he could do so without danger—no one understood him when he spoke. He figured that he'd lost his diction and his ability to properly modulate his voice. Without too much sadness he resigned himself to gestures—he'd never had much to say anyway.

A drop of saliva falling on the back of his hand brought him back to the stranger, who was looking with horror at Tuone's open mouth. Closing it carefully to avoid hurting his gums, he wiped off the drool with his left sleeve and got up from his rock. He nodded his head and called the sheep with a whistle whose shrillness he could not hear. He was climbing the hill, his back to the orange horizon of the sea, when he felt the visitor's hand on his shoulder. He turned around and looked at him with absolute patience. The man repeated the same series of gestures and, sliding his eyeglasses up to his forehead, took from his pocket a piece of paper with something written on it, which he then held out in front of Tuone's eyes. Udina raised his arms to signify that he didn't know how to read, then continued walking uphill. Now and again he turned around—upon reaching the highest part of the hill; as he changed direction to take the dirt track that separated the olive groves from the vineyards; when passing through the gate into the barnyard—to confirm that the visitor was following a few steps behind him, staring obstinately at the ground.

While he was checking the barn door he decided to confront the man, if he was, in fact, still waiting for him, so he strode out decisively to the edge of the barnyard and faced him with his arms crossed, either to extract an explanation, despite this being, after all, impossible—or perhaps to scare him away. The man pointed to his mouth. Then, opening it and closing it exaggeratedly, he made a rather grotesque show of the action of speaking. Udina calculated that the problem could be eloquently resolved with his fists, but the night had now fallen completely and he could just as easily slip away. He lowered his arms and walked off to the cave that he had lived in during the war. As he approached the woods he quickened his step and managed to lose the stranger.

Early the next morning, the shepherd emerged from the far side of the woods with feline caution. He followed the long path to the farm and took the risk of moving the sheep out through the gate that opened directly onto the main road: the young owner didn't usually come up to visit the fields except on the weekends, so there was little chance of being caught breaking the rules. He followed the rocky path to approach the coastline pastures from the other side. Followed by the sheep, he climbed the flanks of one of the mountains that isolated the place from the rest of the island. From there he made sure that the stranger wasn't waiting for him at the back gate of the field. He continued confidently toward the sea and spent the day in peace, avoiding his rock. Not finding an appropriate lookout from which to watch the declining afternoon, he returned early along his usual path. The stranger was waiting for him, red from the cold, leaning against the ancient stone wall that protected the vineyards. He was wearing the same clothes as the day before, except for his footwear: some army boots that stood out conspicuously beneath the cuffs of his pants. The consequences of the sheep getting into the vineyard or the olive grove were much more serious than putting up with the visitor's gesturing for a little while. So Tuone kept on walking.

The man blocked his way and insisted on speaking with him; he pulled out the same paper, holding it up before Tuone's eyes, and again pointed to his mouth and pantomimed speaking. Tuone waited for him to finish. Then he drew close enough for the man to smell his woodsy odor, and threatened him, shaking his fist before the man's eyeglasses. Against the visitor's face, his heavily lined and calloused hand looked, for a moment, like a tree branch. As if to ward off the blow, the stranger lifted his dainty hooves—rosy pink despite his fingertips bruised purple by the cold—took a step back and pulled out a wad of money from inside his jacket. The slightly ridiculous color told the shepherd right away that it was Italian money. He lowered his fist: perhaps now they could understand one another.

The visitor took one of the bills and held it out to Udina, putting the rest of the money into his pants pocket. The shepherd took the bill and studied it skeptically. He knew that in Rijeka they accepted both lire and marks, but he couldn't distinguish between the different denominations. Then the man picked up a stone from the ground, pointed to it and mimed the action of speaking. As Udina didn't react, he opened and closed his fingers, making the shape of a duck's bill, and patted the outside of the pocket where he had put the other money. Tuone thought a little, then barely murmured the word "stone." The visitor froze like a rabbit, his eyes open wide behind his glasses. A smile formed beneath his mustache, he took out another bill, gave it to the islander, and pointed again to the stone. Udina repeated the word a little more carefully; the man gave him a third bill and a pat on the shoulder. The shepherd pointed to the road leading to the farmhouse and the sheep that were already starting to wander away again. His visitor nodded and made a gesture that Udina interpreted as an invitation to meet there again the next morning. Neither one of the two was moved to touch the other to say good-bye: they both raised their hands, the stranger cordially and the islander somewhat clumsily, the branches of his fingers barely flexible in that moment of civility.

Between the third and fourth days of the Italian's visit, Tuone Udina made more money than he had earned in his whole life. The professor pointed to some object and Tuone said a word, first as he remembered having pronounced it in his youth, and then slowly, sound by sound. Sometimes he had to repeat it several times, slowly or quickly. When the visitor felt satisfied, he made a note of it and gave away some more money. Then he flipped through his notebook—the pages fluttering in the wind—or laboriously wrote down the new term on the piece of paper that he had showed Tuone days before.

The lire and the shepherd's good will came to an end at the same time. The visitor thanked him with exaggerated gestures and acted out a little play that was meant to signify his return in a few weeks with more money and a doctor who would heal his gums. The most challenging part of the message was showing the passage of time: in his pantomime, he slept and woke up several times in a row. Udina understood from the first moment but pretended not to so he could enjoy the twisted pleasure of watching a city dweller throw himself to the ground, clap his palms together and place them under his cheek like a pillow, close his eyes, open them, then get back up and do it all over again.

When he returned to his office at the Museum of Archaeology in Rome, Professor Spazzola took his time organizing the information he had gathered on the island. Tuone Udina, the last speaker of Dalmatian, was not only a biological disaster, he was also a mental disgrace. In the scarcely sixteen hours they'd spent together, the shepherd had systematically and diametrically varied the nouns that Spazzola, with seeming carelessness, asked him to repeat from one day to the next. Nothing, or almost nothing, in the few grammatically acceptable expressions that he managed to coax out of him, showed any consistency at all. The majority of the sounds Udina emitted were indistinguishable due to the atrophy of his vocal cords, the impossibility of articulating consonants through his swollen gums, and his basic stupidity. There had been no correspondence—however remote—between his vocal production and the few documents that the Dalmatian rulers produced in the twelfth and thirteenth centuries, when they had the opportunity to govern the territory granted them by Rome. The professor had taken one of them with him, copied in modern script in the hope that the shepherd—about whose state of health he had not been notified before the trip—might possibly have learned the alphabet during his childhood in Veglia, which had then been the last bastion of that most defenseless of Romance languages.

Despite everything, the professor was able to resolve some of his doubts about the survival of Latinate vocalization in Illyria. A certain liberality of reflection permitted him to overcome the narrow limits of his frustration and so publish, with great fanfare, an article in a world-renowned Viennese philological journal. A round of conferences—with a decidedly nationalist focus—on the university circuit served him well by spreading through the newspapers the fear of a Romance language becoming extinct, and thus alerting the government. Under the auspices of a gala dinner, the Ministry of Antiquities secured the funds necessary to rescue the last living speaker of Dalmatian from Austro-Hungarian ignorance and oppression and bring him to the imperial city that had once, with greater wisdom, governed the lives of his ancestors.

Tuone Udina never in the least expected that his visitor would return to keep the promise of helping get his gums cured, for which reason he saved the lire for some special moment when he would really need them, and he forgot all about the matter. He put the money in a wooden box and buried it in the back of his cave.

One Saturday, after penning up the sheep, the shepherd saw that his boss was waiting for him outside the barn with a huge smile on his face and a letter in his hand. Tuone returned his smile, bowed his head, and tried to avoid him to go running back to his cave: rich people's happiness had never brought good news to the island of Veglia. The owner caught up with him, took him by the arm, and showed him the letter, patting him on the back. It was hard for Tuone to believe that the letter was for him—he'd never received one before—much less that the professor was going to return and take him back with him to Italy. The idea that they had already set up a room for him inside the Museum of Archaeology in Rome was beyond belief. His boss didn't tire of repeating the idea—although he knew that it would never get through to his servant—that of all the inhabitants of the Dalmatian archipelago, it was none other than Tuone Udina who was going to spend the rest of his days living in a palace. After letting the shepherd go on his way, he went into the farmhouse and wrote a reply, saying that they had received the news with pleasure, and that they would be happy to accept some reasonable compensation for losing their most loyal worker. He took care to add that, if it had not been for his father's charity, the Dalmatian language would have become extinct during the internecine war of 1878.

For some time, Tuone continued to follow the routine of his shepherd's life. Restricted by the vegetative condition of his fingers, he stayed in his cave until after the sun rose. When he summoned the energy to go and take out the sheep, the dizzying possibility of abandoning the island left him stuck on his rock, even in the scorching midday heat. By the week of the professor's expected return he'd gathered the courage necessary to make his departure. Then, for the first time in twenty years, he decided to take a day off work. If he was going on a trip, it would be best that he cross over to Rijeka and buy himself some new army boots like the ones he'd seen his visitor wearing.

He dug up his lire, then left the cave and the woods along the little-used path that led directly to the coast. Passing by his rock, he crossed the sheep's favorite valley. When he reached the promontory from which the coastline was visible, he saw in the distance that the stevedores were already loading the first ferry of the day. The prospect of waiting until the second trip, at midafternoon, without anything to do, impelled him to save the time it would take to go through the coves by cutting across the mountain along the cliff. He was certain that he was going to reach the dock on time when, crossing one of the fields that crowned the heights, he felt the earth give way beneath his feet. It took him a moment to realize that he had slipped into a hole. He couldn't hear the sharp click of the detonator that was activated the moment he touched bottom.

ON THE DEATH OF THE AUTHOR

> Your face is inscribed in my soul.
> And how much I long to write of you.

GARCILASO DE LA VEGA

Some stories are, seemingly, impossible to tell. It must be at least ten years since I took a trip through California, and since then I've been trying to write, without the least success, the story of a particular grand finale: it's the story of Ishi, a Yahi Indian who was discovered in his aboriginal condition in the remote ranching town of Oroville in August 1910.

I'd always wanted to take a trip that would begin in Cabo San Lucas, the southernmost point of the Californias, and wind up in whatever was its northernmost city, which turned out to be Oroville. On that trip, as I imagined it, my ex-wife and I would drive from south to north as if navigating some beat poet's dream, and we would see amazing things, stop in impossibly sinister places, and talk to some free-spirited—and frankly bizarre—characters.

Unfortunately, things didn't turn out that way. First, our trip by car through most of California began at the halfway mark—at the Los Angeles airport. Second, we weren't cruising in a black Cadillac loaded with a stash of drugs, each more powerful than the last—instead we were driving an especially hellish minivan, in the not ungrateful, and hardly unbearable, company of my wife's two grandmothers.

Although the diary of our trip doesn't offer much in the way of literary fodder, it had its interesting moments, for example when we showed the grandmothers how to nullify some spicy chili peppers at a Chinese restaurant by dipping the tips in salt, or when one of them read a book of Ferlinghetti's poems that I'd brought along to feel like a true beat, and said that she liked them. We also saw a photo exhibit about Ishi at the University Museum at Cal Berkeley.

The story of the last Indian in the United States living in a pure, untainted condition shouldn't be a difficult one to tell, nor would it seem to conceal any unavoidable pitfalls for anyone ardently devoted to relating certain things while meaning others. But there's something in the tale—or inside me—that makes it elusive: I've tried the pastiche technique, direct narration, diary entries, epistolary form, even the dreaded stream of consciousness, but the whole thing keeps slipping through my fingers like a fistful of marbles.

The facts are simple and transparent: early one morning, a group of workers found a man collapsed on the doorstep of a slaughterhouse, dying from starvation and exhaustion. They carried him inside the building and gave him water. Then they noticed that he was a wild Indian, something that made no sense, under the circumstances, but which their parents and grandparents had taught them to identify as an enemy. They tied his hands and feet—as if he were really capable of escaping—and sent for the sheriff.

The officer in question, perhaps the last Wild West cowboy still working for the government in that part of the United States, threw the Indian over the back of his horse, just as he was, and took him to jail, not because he wanted to make him suffer but because he didn't know what else to do with him—at least that's what he told the press. For the record, it seems that he dressed Ishi in his own clothes, and fed him food that his wife cooked especially so that the Indian wouldn't die of hunger before he was turned over to the army, which was what the sheriff figured he was bound to do with him.

By midday, the news of the discovery had sped like a burning fuse through the whole area, so that a memorably tumultuous crowd gathered at the jail for a glimpse of the last savage in the United States. Among those that filed past his cell was a San Francisco newspaper correspondent, who dispatched a feverish wire describing the sheriff's highly extraordinary negotiations between his own impassioned citizens—still nursing wounds from the long-ended Indian wars in that region—and the various owners of vaudeville shows that wanted to buy the Indian and add him to their slate of attractions.

Luckily for Ishi, who would've died had the sheriff been less honest or the army faster in coming to seize him and drag him off to a reservation, the story in the San Francisco newspaper was read by a professor. When the man noticed that nobody could understand the Indian's language, he deduced that Ishi must be a speaker of Yana, a supposedly extinct language for which a friend of his was compiling a glossary.

The professor caught the first train to Oroville and, armed with his colleague's notes about the Yahis' language, went and rescued Ishi. Once back in San Francisco, he realized that, while saving the Indian, he hadn't considered the problem of where to lodge him. So, although his own brand of logic seems even crazier than either Ishi's or the sheriff's, he obeyed what it whispered in his ear and brought him to the Museum of Anthropology.

In the days following these events, there was some discussion about what to do with Ishi, but finally everyone agreed that the best place for the last surviving aborigine in the United States was, ultimately, a museum. Ishi spent the rest of his life there, much more comfortable and seemingly more satisfied than if he had been out in the woods. At first he lived in the guest rooms, then in the staff quarters, and at last in the sunniest of the exhibition rooms. There they set up a bed for him so that he could die from tuberculosis in peace and comfort three years after surrendering to white people.

It's probably true that this story's power is located simply in the events themselves; trying to articulate its meaning always ends up making it seem like cheap sentiment, or, worse yet, a parable of virtuous political intentions; the lowest sort of affectation, guaranteed. To spin metaphors out of a story that means something on its own terms is like being in love with love: however powerful it might seem at first, it always turns out badly.

Whichever way you want to read it, the story of the man who earned his living as a museum piece always seemed fascinating and revealing to me, mostly due to the fact that, despite everything, despite all the good and seemingly honest friends he made among the community of doctors and anthropologists who studied him, the Indian never wanted to tell them his real name. Until the last day of his life he always asked them to call him Ishi, which in Yana means "Man": apparently, when one is the last surviving example of something, the name of the species suffices.

I'm increasingly convinced that the problem with Ishi's story is one of literalness: it means what it means and not what I want it to mean.

Three years ago, when I was still living in Washington, D.C. and had just turned thirty, I decided to take a Sunday off from the hellish move I was making to Boston, where I now live. It's not that I was nostalgic, exactly, about quitting the nation's capital; I'd spent some good years there but the last ones had been pretty depressing. I simply felt like say-ing good-bye to the city where I'd finished growing up, in which my ex-wife and children were going to stay with the vague promise that the four of us would live together again once our jobs permitted it, and that this time things would work out. During a pathetic evening out on the town—a sham of everything that we'd lost—we went to have dinner at our favorite restaurant and afterward to a place with a patio and French pretensions, which at that time served the best coffee in D.C.

We were eating cheesecake for dessert, each of us con-centrating on playing our assigned role, when along came a redhead, striding between the tables with the self-assurance of an avenging angel. She was wearing a T-shirt emblazoned with the word *Redhead.* When I saw her, I felt sure that such literalness could infect the world with the same type of metaphysical disequilibrium that dominates some novels by Eça de Queiroz: each time that redhead puts on that T-shirt which says *Redhead*, I told my ex-wife, an Indian in Mexico dies. I think she got my joke, or got it well enough, because on the last trip I made to Mexico, I'd brought back a T-shirt as a gag gift, which read: *Eres un pendejo,* "You're an idiot." Below that, in parentheses: (*You are my friend*).

Of course, I don't really believe that a Mexican Indian dies each time the redhead wears her *Redhead* T-shirt, but it does seem to me that such literalness can end up being nox-ious, although I'm not quite sure for what.

Or maybe I do: noxious for oneself. I know from experi-ence that the literal can be really bad luck. Not long after having made such a snide remark about that idiot (friend) in the T-shirt in that D.C. café, I went to give a series of readings in Berlin. I've suffered some memorable disasters thanks to these types of event: for one reason or another, some kind of weirdo always decides to attend the talk you're giving, no matter how boring or unbearable the topic. If fame is what you're after, reading a story or an excerpt from a novel in public is usually a lesson in why one shouldn't be a writer.

Berlin consisted of three public appearances. The first was a roundtable on some of those open-vein themes that help Europeans and gringos of good conscience feel really fine about themselves but which make us Latin Americans who are invited to participate feel more like artifacts on display in a compassion museum. There were also two proper literary readings: one was in a theater, with something of an actual audience—it was free, it was raining, and there was wine—and the other was in a café that seemed like it must have been highly fashionable when East Berlin was still communist. The café was called Einstein, to which was added the strange qualifier *Under the Lindens*.

The name of the place stood out to me the first time I read it listed on my schedule of appearances in the German capital, but it left me with a sense of deep foreboding when, the next morning, while practicing the worst kind of tourism in the neighborhood around the Brandenburg Gate, I found myself right in front of the place. It turned out that its strange "subtitle" came from its indeed being located on a street—similar to La Rambla in Barcelona—called Unter den Linden precisely because it runs beneath some linden trees.

I was born in a city, Mexico City, where there's an overgrown forest without any wild animals called "Desert of the Lions"; for this reason, the Adamic Teuton imagination, so very humorless, gave me the chills. My nephew, whose name is Jorge Arrieta, summed it up with all the crystal clarity of his eight years during an argument with one of my kids. It was last August and the three of us had gone to my parents' house for a vacation that turned out to be so unpleasant we had to cut it short: That game, he spat, is about as much fun as playing Call Yourself Jorge Arrieta.

In any event, in that café called *Einstein Under the Lindens* I had the worst experience that one can have in such cases: it wasn't a totally empty house; exactly two ticket holders showed up, so that the moderator, the translator, the actor who was going to read my story in German, and I all crowded round a table at the front of an auditorium that felt like the loneliest ship on the seas, inhabited as it was by only a young woman and her mother. Not only did we still have to read, we did the whole roundtable routine—complete with simultaneous translations—because the two women had paid, and in a city where a street that runs under linden trees is called "Under the Lindens," you deliver the fifty-minute show that you promised.

Ishi never lacked for a public: four days a week he gave a presentation in the reception hall of the museum during which he sang some ritual song, kindled a fire by rubbing two sticks together, and showed the visitors how to fashion bows and arrows with materials brought from the canyons near Oroville. These things were delivered to him there in the museum—despite the anthropologists' insistence, he didn't want to return to his homeland. Two other days of the week he spent dusting and mopping all the rooms in the museum, except for one of them containing an exhibit of mummies and funeral offerings that Ishi always refused to enter. On Mondays he would usually head out early to take the streetcar down to the sea.

It wasn't until the last summer of his life that he agreed, with great reluctance, and perhaps because he felt that he had little time left, to return to the canyons: in August of

1913 he went with his doctor and the museum director to recreate the life in the wild that he had led until the moment he'd surrendered at the slaughterhouse. The three of them spent several wonderful days living naked in the outdoors, eating whatever they could hunt in the forest.

The original idea was to stay there for a whole month, but Ishi insisted that they return to San Francisco; each time that they tried to convince him otherwise, he made it clear that he preferred the comfort of the museum over returning to live in the wilderness. Apparently, it never occurred to anyone to consider that returning to the forest might be depressing for the Indian. During what the doctor calculated to have been his first thirty-three years of life, Ishi hadn't exactly been living in a rose garden.

The Yahi tribe was the last in the United States to be subjugated: unlike in the cases of the Apache or the Lakota, there was no formal surrender process because the Yahi were exterminated with singular viciousness: if the federal troops discovered them before the bands of trackers that set out from Oroville, they would take them to a reservation, but no white person from the area seemed to consider that punishment enough.

Ishi survived because he had the unheard of luck of not being present during either one of his tribe's two fatal encounters with the enemy. In the first, the Indian hunters—relatively civilized family men when they were not scouring the hills—happened one afternoon upon the last remaining Yahi camp in the canyons. The tribe had already been devastated by five years of war and persecution—and the hunters waited patiently for daybreak to be able to fire on them from the hilltops. Ishi had gone to the forest with his grandmother who, it seems, was the tribe's shaman, and they had spent the night there so the evening dew might bless the roots they had gathered. Upon returning, they found the camp destroyed. It took them some time to locate the rest of the tribe, who were left almost without any men: the women and the children had taken cover in the gullies while the braves sacrificed themselves to the ranchers' gunfire. From their refuge in the mountains, the surviving Yahis went foraging and hunting by night.

One day, a band of white men, aware that some of the enemy had escaped them, found a trail of deer blood under the trees—which in all likelihood were lindens. They followed it and had no problem discovering the Yahis' hiding place. According to a superbly written account by one of the hunters, the situation was ideal: having occupied the mouth of a dead-end cave, none of the Indians was able to escape. In one of the tale's most shocking passages, the California gentleman relates that at one point during the massacre he decided to use his revolver because it made for a cleaner job: babies, he quickly learned, explode when you shoot them with a rifle.

I only found out that part of Ishi's story later on—a part that he never knew well, or never with the same detail I now know it—in a book of chronicles from the period at my university's library. For his part, he simply returned with his mother and his sister from the creek and found that, for the second time, they had to start burying their dead. Although he never spoke directly about that day, he alluded more than once to the terrible task of having to bury all of his people.

By the time I read that account I'd already tried five or six times, without the least success, to write a story about Ishi, and it always turned out to be too political: deadly literal with all its meanings exposed, or not all of them but definitely those that interested me least. What seduces me about Ishi is not his tragic condition and how clearly that reflects the fact that the American continent is the booming utopia of a gang of criminals, but the unimaginable loneliness of one who knows himself to be the last of something, for which no hope remains.

The version that I wrote at that time was the worst of them all, because by then I was loaded down with other humiliations, and consumed, as a result, with the sort of moral outrage that makes us find certain forms of hypocrisy preferable to others. That version of the story was called "Taking Democracy to California." The title alone is bad enough.

There is another story, a very good one, by Bernardo Atxaga, who tells how one day, walking through a town in his native region of the Basque Country, he suddenly found himself facing an old man outside a door with a hole in it. They spoke a little bit and at last the old man asked him if he knew why there was a hole in the door. Atxaga says that he answered that it must be for the cat. No, the man told him, it was made years ago so they could feed a little boy who turned into a dog after being bitten by one.

The stories that I like, the ones that make me jealous and fill me with a wild desire to write ones just like them, have the same dazzling logic as the old Basque man; there's a piece missing, and that gap transforms them into myth. They appeal to the lowest common denominator, which makes us all more or less the same.

If a dog bites a little boy and gives him rabies, the illusion of a universal rule of cause and effect is maintained; order exists, for which reason there are categories. If, on the other hand, the boy turns into a dog, the world is uncontrollable—like our affections, our inability to live up to our own standards, and our undeserved misfortunes, which is to say, almost all of them. Atxaga's friendly old man would never wear a T-shirt that said *Old Man*; his words alone suffice, for the same reason that when writing literature or making movies, the best stories are love stories that go wrong: they're preloaded with everything required for *A* to lead to *B* and from there to little children, but something gets fucked up without anyone knowing what happened, exactly, and so *A* leads to the cliffs of *W* and the *S* curve of suicide.

In spite of the fact that he lived almost his entire life in the most acute loneliness, Ishi always resisted the temptation of killing himself—but the silence of a museum is even worse than that of an unpromising professor's apartment, so that reading about a solitude like Ishi's, which couldn't even derive any pleasure from the chic touch of being self-inflicted, makes me feel something similar to what I was made to feel by reading about the solitude of the boy who turned into a dog. It fills me with the hope that someday the futures that slip through my fingers like marbles will seem like a mythology.

Ishi's third and final misadventure with white people before surrendering at the slaughterhouse in Oroville was the definitive one. Several months went by before he gave himself up, and it reflects what was going to be his final destiny: the lean-to in which he lived with his mother and his sister was discovered by a group of geology professors accompanying a mining expedition. Although they never met face to face, the disorder that the scientists left behind in their camp was sufficient to make the Indians decide to escape to save what remained of their skins. They scattered. Ishi never again saw either his sister or his mother, who probably died a terrible death during their flight, but who surely left this world with the epic aplomb of those who endure without surrender.

Ishi gave himself up because he was trying to find

something to eat, thinking perhaps that if he was going to die one way or other, it was better to do so with a full stomach. Having made that decision paints him as weak, and for those of us who have tried to tell his story it brings us very close to the abyss of literalness. Being the last survivor of an entire world, who also happens to live in a museum, is meaning itself: there are no missing pieces, and without mystery there is no mythology.

It's for that reason, I believe, it is better to imagine him in the days when, instead of being an Indian in a glass display case, he was only the densest of the museum's custodians. One must think of him resigned to be the last of something, and thus mopping the hallways in a state of holy calm.

A few months after Ishi arrived in San Francisco, the problem arose that, because of museum regulations, he couldn't live in the guest rooms forever. So they decided to make him a maintenance worker and pay him a salary so that he could live with the staff. To everyone's surprise, he didn't understand that it was all about solving the problem of his being the last of something and there being nowhere to keep him. The next day he put on some worker's coveralls and asked for a bucket.

He used almost no money, except for buying a few things to eat, always simple: honey, corn meal, squash, apples, coffee: he was a very small man and notoriously frugal. He also spent some money taking the trolley car from Golden Gate Park out to see the ocean. He spent all his days off there: the sea is the place where we forgive ourselves for the marbles that slipped through our fingers without our understanding why. The rest of his wages he saved up in the safe at the museum: he kept the money in some boxes for medicine ampules that his doctor gave him, each of which had the exact size, shape, and width to snugly hold ten silver-dollar coins. At the end of his life he became fond of staring at them: he would ask the director to open the safe for him; he would set his boxes of dollars on a table and spend the afternoon looking at them, without ever saying anything or taking the coins out. As if they were something else.

If one is the last of something, his hoardings are not savings, but the balance of an entire universe: we find it there, in Ishi's untellable story, when the bitten boy turns into a dog, the forest is called "Desert," and the redheaded girl wears a T-shirt that doesn't say *pendeja.*

Sometimes writing is a job: obliquely tracing the path of certain ideas that seem indispensable to us, that we have to set down. But other times it's a question of conceding what remains, accepting the museum and contemplating the balance while awaiting death, asking forgiveness of the sea for whatever was fucked up. Placing our little boxes on the table and knowing that what came to an end was also the whole universe.

Two Waltzes Toward Civilization

After this we'll know how to eat against death, to
devour only dead things, cooking to kill them again.
We'll know that feeding means dealing with other
bodies, that desire makes us itch, and it only finds
relief in order to get worse, that to love is to devour.

ANTONIO JOSÉ PONTE

ESCAPE FROM SUICIDE CITY

I leave the Soul behind; bearing onward,
my pilgrim body, deserted and alone.

QUEVEDO

I

Mr. Hinojosa was waiting for me outside the Lima airport in the sinister black Mercedes Benz the Swiss television producer had rented to pick up the guests for *Lard*, the highly successful European TV cooking show that had been a minor cable hit in the United States and Canada.

Although I'd heard some of my colleagues express their admiration, and even reverence, for the program, I never watched it because I don't own a TV. My own gastronomic principles require me to live in total retreat from the world; I don't believe that one can recreate seventeenth-century Mexican conventual cooking unless one exists in harmony with the ways of life that gave rise to it.

This vision that I've nurtured my entire life was by no means easy to make a reality, especially because my restaurant is located in Washington, D.C., the world's most shameless city, with its ten-foot-wide sidewalks, its streets the size of soccer fields, and its monuments standing as an architectural prelude to national obesity. Nevertheless, it was here that I found a financier to invest in my talents, and I do what I can to recreate those customs and conditions. Both my sesame honey glazed squid, and my *chilpachole verde*—a spicy green crab soup—have earned me some slight recognition in the pages of the local food section.

The concept behind *Lard* is that six young, promising chefs compete to eliminate each other by passing a series of trials putting to the test their charisma, manners, and hygiene, as well as their ability to improvise with unusual ingredients. The producers film the whole competition—in itself, quite boring—then jazz it up in editing. Each episode takes place in a different location and is judged by a different celebrity from the world of international gastronomy. The broadcast I was invited to was filmed in Lima because the theme was "Latin American Seafood Cuisine" and Max Terapia was the guest star.

Like all chefs of my generation, I admire and envy Terapia, although I realize that I'm never going to achieve his level of celebrity: when his star began to rise, in the '60s, Latin American cuisine enjoyed no international cachet, while European cuisine was still trapped in the excessive experimentation that characterized that decade. So, thanks to his creations, as fine and transparent as a razor blade, he scooped up all the prizes and honors without any competition. They called him the master of gastronomy *povera*, an authentic revolutionary in an eminently bourgeois art. These days he's based in Miami, where he owns a restaurant catering to an exclusive clientele and which is only open during the cooler months of the year. The place has neither a name nor a front door; you enter by car, through a rolling metal shutter at the rear of the building. Terapia spends the rest of his time as a guest chef at important, high-level culinary events, and at his nineteenth-century house in the center of Lima, which is said to have, and which I confirmed, its original kitchen intact, with a stove that burns charcoal and guano, a cool room, and a hand-powered water pump. A kitchen, it must be said, on account of which I'm almost dying with envy. All my silent partner would pay to have

146

installed in my own place was a bread oven and a wood-fired grill; he told me to buckle down, get busy, and use them to make something wonderful, which I've never stopped trying to do since Teresa left me years ago, and I turned my back on the world.

The Swiss, it seems, are naturally mysterious. One day, an enormous glossy envelope arrived at my office. Inside it was a signed letter from some enigmatic Secretariat, informing me that I'd been nominated to compete in *Lard*. I answered them the very same day, that I was quite honored to receive their invitation but that I had no idea what *Lard* was—of course I knew, but I wanted to keep them on their toes—and could they do me the favor of explaining things to me. I said that I'd be grateful if they could tell me who'd nominated me so that I could thank them: as far as I know, the only people who eat at my restaurant are Adams Morgan residents and a few Mexican diplomats and professors who tend to be excessively nostalgic—as if the food that I make really has something in common with the country that we were all so happy to escape from.

The same, mysterious Secretariat answered with another extremely pompous letter, along with a promotional flyer for the program, informing me that under no circumstances could they reveal the identity of their advisory committee. In the coming weeks a new panel of connoisseurs would visit my restaurant—they would make the final decision about who would and who wouldn't take part in *Lard*.

Again I requested more precise information, to be sure that we would treat the visiting committee well when it showed up. They replied by saying that the anonymity of the visit was sacrosanct. I felt humiliated, and in one of those crazy, headstrong moments that make us lose World Cup games we've already won by committing fouls, I demanded that they at least tell me who my competition would be. Another giant envelope from the Secretariat, another refusal.

I've lost too many contests—including one that was rigged in my favor—for the likelihood of my being judged to keep me awake at night. Even so, I was on the alert for several weeks, awaiting the arrival at my restaurant of a contingent of Swiss gentlemen—tall, balding, red-faced, and wearing thick eyeglasses. In the fantasies produced by my abominably boring and friendless life, in an apartment without a TV, that's precisely how the Swiss appear.

Nobody who looked even remotely like that ever sat down at our tables, so I supposed that they'd forgotten about me, or that the Swiss might have snuck in in the guise of gringo students or Mexican office clerks. One of my waiters—a Colombian know-it-all—told me that the Swiss were Calvinists, and that's how we'd be able to recognize them. I asked him what a Calvinist would look like. He told me that they're very strict, practically vegetarians, and that they've got no lips. I took note.

At last a woman with a neutral French accent phoned to let me know that my masterful red snapper in fig vinaigrette had earned me the privilege of competing on *Lard*. She didn't speak Spanish but she understood my English, and she was polite, friendly, and obviously very young. It had never occurred to me that there were also Swiss women, much less ones that were young. She was quite insistent that it was the fine quality of my cooking that had won me the honor of participating, that I should be proud and list it as such on my résumé, for which reason I supposed my restaurant to be lacking in hygiene and me in charisma. I asked her if she was from the Secretariat. She didn't understand and again recommended that I include my status as a finalist on my résumé.

Once in Lima, Mr. Hinojosa was equally unable to set me straight. The moment I got in his Mercedes I asked him about the people who had hired him. He said that he had no information to give me. He worked for a security agency and all they told him was what to do—he'd spent the whole day delivering foreigners to a hotel in Miraflores. I spoke vaguely about how Mexican chauffeurs made more money from tips than from their nominal wages, then after a pause asked him if he wasn't *authorized* to give me that information or if he really didn't know. Although I've lived in the United States for several years, I know perfectly well how to overcome the resistance of my fellow Latin Americans. He told me that if he knew he would tell me because he liked me. Sure, I answered him. Are you attending a conference? he asked me after a while. I was riding along staring distractedly out the window—I'm from Mexico City but still managed to be astonished by the ugliness of Lima, which even surpassed its reputation. No, I told him, with my eyes fixed on the horrific casinos that lined the avenue down which we traveled, we're here for a dinner, and then a kind of competition.

The program that they'd sent me once I became a finalist wasn't very clear, at least not to me, and if there's something I know nothing about, it's how the media works: the first day was for individual preproduction filming with each chef, then we were all attending a dinner together at the house of Max Terapia—though he was not expected to be cooking. The next day, the actual competition would be filmed at a studio, they'd pay us our honoraria and a cash prize for the winner, then send us home.

It's all a little mysterious, Mr. Hinojosa told me. Normally, people tell me why they've come to Lima, but you're the fifth one that I've picked up today and only the first to tell me anything. Is it a conference for secret agents? he asked. I told him it wasn't, that it was for chefs. Another one of the envelopes that I'd gotten after talking with the perky young Swiss woman contained an astonishingly long contract that forbade me from saying anything about my participating in *Lard* save to my most discreet, intimate associates. I supposed, however, that the clause was really there to prevent my saying anything to food critics and other chefs, so I saw no reason not to tell Mr. Hinojosa that I was going to a dinner at Max Terapia's house. He slammed on the brakes, screeching to a halt in the middle of the street, then turned around to face me. Is he here in Lima? he asked me, as if the presence in town of a saucepan artiste was something of great import. He looked out the windows, nervously glancing left and right. I suppose so, I told him, then continued, a bit astonished: Do you really know who Max Terapia is? Shifting into first gear, he answered me with the air of a man well versed in conspiracies: If you mean the same man who's cooked for kings and popes, of course I do. The look on his face as he shifted into second seemed to indicate that we were both members of some secret fraternity. He's the Peruvian cosmopolitan *par excellence*, he continued, the closest thing that we've still got to Chabuca Granda, although all the *cholo* trash around here who resent him are just jealous. *Cholos?* I asked him, unable to suppress a note of irony: Peruvians use the term *cholo* for the lowest, most dispossessed Indians, and Mr. Hinojosa himself must have had at least ninety percent indigenous blood. Peru is full of Indians, as you people call them, he answered me. As we call them? You're Mexican, if I'm not mistaken. I live in the United States, I told him, immediately recognizing how, thanks to my losing a grievous emotional duel with myself, I'd compromised my principles by seeking refuge in the arms of the enemy.

We spent the rest of the drive in silence: Mr. Hinojosa now making himself the mysterious one—twirling the world's rattiest little mustache, checking each intersection with low, sidelong glances—and me thinking that during my first thirty minutes in Lima I'd established a rapport with this stranger that was much deeper than any I'd developed during my four years *à la gringo*. And why did you move to the United States? he asked me all at once, with terrifying acuity. I answered that I did it for the same reason everyone did, for the money, and he seemed satisfied with that explanation. At a certain moment—by now we were near the hotel—he took a shortcut along a side street so that we'd pass by the ruins of a pre-Columbian military post, which was lit up at night. I was sure that he was going to kidnap me until we reached a dead-end street at whose end rose a man-made hill, which was really quite beautiful. Perhaps still on the defensive, I asked him if the Incas were *cholo* trash too. He didn't understand the refined sarcasm of my question, or he understood it too well, because he answered me that the ruins weren't exactly Incan, that the Inca were condors, winged monsters. The children of the sun, he said with a wholly unself-conscious nostalgia.

Once at the hotel, after agreeing that he'd take me back to the airport on the following Sunday at five o'clock in the afternoon—I kept insinuating that he'd receive his tip then—he offered me his hand and I shook it with a vigor that I never use in D.C. I thought then that if he'd invited me for a few beers I might have roused myself to tell him how Teresa had run off with one of my history students, one whom I had personally helped to secure a scholarship at the University of Chicago.

Another luxurious envelope awaited me in my hotel

room—this time handwritten with a fountain pen, on equally expensive paper—welcoming me and issuing the threat that I'd have to eat breakfast at seven A.M. because the makeup people were arriving at eight o'clock and the six different production teams would depart a half-hour later to film the guest chefs in various sequences around Lima. Alongside the letter was a box of chocolates and a lavishly printed catalog that related the amazing history of *Lard*. As I leafed through it I was able to recognize other chefs who, like me, were born in the '60s, and I felt retrospectively offended for not having been invited to the program until so late in life. I went downstairs to the bar to have a whiskey and something to eat before going to bed. There were no bald, lipless, red-faced men in sight, which seemed natural enough to me: Calvinists go to bed early.

At last it turned out that the Swiss did indeed look like gringo students, albeit without lips: my Colombian waiter, it seems, really does know it all. When I went downstairs at seven thirty the next morning, the hotel restaurant was already crowded with people—it had been years since I'd gotten up at such an insulting hour, perhaps not since the remote but haunting days when I'd been a history professor, watched television, and lived with Teresa in Mexico. The majority of the tables were occupied by regular tourists, but in the back of the room there was a group to which I obviously belonged: five tables, each one with two gringo students and a Latin American one, and then a sixth with only two students, which was obviously my table. I introduced myself there with the same sense of ennui that permits us artists to live so barbarously without ever paying the consequences. My producer was the young Swiss woman with the neutral French accent whom I'd spoken to on the telephone. She told me very cordially and efficiently that we

152

had to hurry up if we wanted to film all the necessary foot-age, then she introduced herself and the cameraman who would be accompanying us. He was red-faced and blond, but he had a spectacular mass of hair between his head and his neck, and to be honest, more ennui than I did. I told them there was no problem, that I only drank coffee for breakfast—a lie—and as I looked around for a waiter, I took advantage of the moment to sneak a glance at the competi-tion. None of the faces—each of which offered me a hostile glance—seemed familiar.

I had exactly fifteen minutes to get halfway acquainted with what we were going to do and to take three sips of my coffee. At seven forty-five people began heading up to their rooms to brush their teeth. At eight o'clock they combed and brushed our hair, got us into makeup in the hotel salon, where they also gave us some general instructions, and at eight thirty each group departed for its filming.

While they were getting us ready, I was unable to talk with any of the other chefs: they seated us well away from each other, whether to avoid friction or to keep us from com-municating with each other I don't know. I was constantly flanked by my producer and my cameraman. One chef—his height and hair suggested he might be Argentine—gave me a look that suggested that it was ridiculous to put up with such things. I spotted the other Mexican right away by his pointed loafers and impossible hair. He gave me a nasty look, partly as a result of the fact that he knew I was better than him and partly because if there's one thing that people can't stand, it's when one of their compatriots gains a bit of recognition outside their country.

When the chief producer finished giving us the neces-sary instructions for the rest of the day, they started calling us individually, and we headed out, each tightly surrounded by our crew, straight to the parking area. There, six mini-vans awaited us, in which we departed the hotel one by one, like children heading out on a scavenger hunt. Descending into the hazy light of Lima and seeing by day how much it resembled Mexico City, I had the dizzy feeling of a Spanish speaker who hears Portuguese for the first time: you feel like you should understand it but something is out of place; it's your language and it's not your language—a parallel reality. I was coming back to a place that seemed like home but just wasn't.

II

The truth is that once alone together inside the minivan, my Swiss companions turned out to be fine, warmhearted people. We went along the whole way chatting about everyday things, almost having fun. Every so often they revealed some detail about my life—my time spent in Christian Brothers schools, for example—or they quoted something I'd said in some old interview. They left me with the impression that they knew everything about me while I knew nothing about them: another dream, like the city of Lima itself, sprawling out with all its traffic and all its ugliness, behind which hid a sweetness that was only now becoming apparent to me.

Our first round of filming took place in a convent in the center of Lima. We spent hours shooting scenes in the cloister—one take after another, visits to the kitchen, exhaustive close-ups panning along the library shelves, moments of meditation in the refectory; all of it an atrocious pretense, tacky affectation.

The producer counted down from ten to three, then signaled the final numbers with her fingers, and I feigned the kind of distraction of which I'm fully capable—but not with a cameraman breathing down my neck and a gaggle of little Peruvian girls following us everywhere. I suppose that I'd never had so much attention in my whole life and I probably never would again. Even so, I couldn't stop thinking about the days I'd spent digging up old recipes from the General National Archive in Mexico. I would have traded all those staring faces, which looked so much like success— the little girls' curiosity, the cyclopean eye of the camera— for one second of the enormous attention Teresa once paid me as I expounded on the finer points of Mexican convent life in the seventeenth century, and cooked my colonial concoctions just for her.

We did additional shoots, similar to the one at the convent, at three other fairly important locations around Lima: the train station for the Cuzco line, a beach resort in Barranco, and the Parque del Amor, where the Swiss were horrified to see young couples in the shadows of the trees making out and groping each other with truly impressive inventiveness.

At the train station, the cameraman suggested some refreshment. I was faint from hunger, so it seemed like a magnificent idea. I could already taste my beer and whatever we were going to order for a snack when I saw that the Swiss woman had ordered water, nothing else. I looked at the cameraman with desperation and he looked back with the same. I ordered another coffee. We finished our "snack" in five minutes flat and then continued filming. I promised myself that once I got back to D.C. I'd give my Colombian waiter a raise.

On the way from the train station to the Parque del Amor I noticed how strange the façade was on the only really tall building—in no way did it qualify as a skyscraper—in the center of Lima. The cameraman pointed it out to me: it's dark gray, made of concrete, without decorations or markings, like my life; a true visual nullity, an almost non-space with that very somber look one associates with the headquarters of some sort of secret police. I asked the driver what it was. He became quite serious and told me, in a very low, conspiratorial tone of voice, that it was the Suicide Building. What? I said to him. Those are the Ministry of Commerce offices, he explained to me, but they had to close them to the public because people would go up to the roof and jump off. Look up there at the top, he pointed with his finger, they put up a fence. It didn't do any good, though—after they installed it people would take the elevator up to the ninth or tenth floor and jump out any window they found open.

I asked him with genuine interest if the suicide rate in Lima was very high. Extremely high, he told me with a sadness I did not expect. When they closed the Ministry of Commerce to the public, he continued, people started jumping off a new bridge across the Miraflores ravine. We were rounding a traffic circle, making the Suicide Building appear to turn away, revolving on an axis counter to our own, like a disgraced planet. My field of vision was moving past it, every moment further beyond the façade. I asked him if it could be the economic crisis, remembering that when I first started going out with Teresa everybody in Mexico was losing their job, so there was a net increase in the number of people who threw themselves in front of Metro trains. No, he told me, the ones who've got no money just steal, or they shoot themselves. The ones who jump do it because of love.

I caused a minor scandal during lunch by ordering normal-sized portions of food for a healthy adult; even worse, I drank two beers. It was a seafood restaurant located across the street from the wharf. We ate on the second floor, which had a view of the ocean. All the locals from Lima—businessmen, office workers having affairs, leisurely young millionaires—were eating lunch downstairs, watching the parking lot and the street, ignoring the heaving, steel-colored sea that was, perhaps, too menacing for their fragile, decadent, Creole aplomb. The crowded tables, the cut of the suits, the gelled and sprayed hairdos, the waiters conscious of their inferior birth, all reminded me again of Mexico.

The Swiss ordered a plate of ceviche to share between the three of us, and a salad for each; to drink, water. I couldn't hold back any longer, so I went for a second dish, simple with plenty of food: grilled fish served over puréed potatoes, with a caper salad on the side. I had to eat quickly so that I could order dessert and coffee before they called for the check and dragged me outside to keep filming.

On our way back to the hotel in Miraflores, toward the end of the afternoon, despite the heavy traffic, a fresh, stiff breeze was blowing in through the car windows. At the corner of one street we came to a bridge connecting the outcroppings on either side of a ravine which led out to the district's local beaches. We were driving slowly, so I was able to see that the bridge crossed over a truly frightening drop. Is this the Suicide Bridge? I asked the driver. He nodded his head. I noticed that one side of the bridge already had a fence, while another was being installed on the opposite side. I had an atrocious attack of vertigo, perhaps because during the conversation that morning I'd imagined the driver was exaggerating—fueled, like all his colleagues, by the morbid trivia disseminated by radio newscasts. They're putting up a fence so people don't jump off anymore, I said, almost to myself. The driver maintained such a grave silence while we crossed the bridge that I imagined it was, for him, a cursed spot: like me, he might have suffered from incurable lovesickness.

It's the *cholo* blood, he said to me when we'd returned to solid ground; to fly away when the earth has lost its dignity, like a condor. I couldn't resist asking him if the Incas were *cholos*. With an indifference that bespoke his empty life, he said that he imagined they were.

III

Once back at the hotel, I barely had time to change my shirt, tie, and jacket for the dinner at Terapia's house, which was the thing that interested me most about the whole trip. Despite dressing in such a terrible hurry, I still ended up getting back down to the reception area late and rather disheveled: the rhythms of a man inhabiting an imaginary seventeenth-century apparently don't mix with those of the lunatic tribes running amok in the clamorous twenty-first.

The other chefs and producers were already sitting in the armchairs by the vestibule leading to the street. For the first time, I noticed that my producer was very good looking. She'd put on a flowered dress and brushed on the very slightest hint of makeup. Her hair, untouched, hung loose.

Swiss women, like their gringo counterparts, have an infantile notion of beauty; they want to be pretty, not lethal. They come from cities untouched by Baroque liturgies, and societies that never enjoyed the dubious privilege of being shaped by the customs of a Bourbon court. They don't know that the body is simply a corpse in the making, that seduction is an assassin's game, that beauty is not bright but monstrous. As Rilke said, it's as much terror as we can endure. It's what the one who falls in love loses because it has to stay here on earth, a pilgrim stripped of its own soul.

But Swiss women aren't birds, and she could never understand the flighty anxiety of lovers from Lima. Like gringos, the Swiss long to be happy, while we Latin Americans aspire to burn, nailed to the axis of piety. I was Teresa's pilgrim, and I couldn't stop wondering if my stay in Lima wouldn't end up turning me into her condor.

I was able to approach, albeit briefly, the presumably Argentine chef, who was speaking with a Venezuelan mulatto. The other three chefs—especially the other Mexican—kept their distance, clinging tightly to their producers out of a crazed desire to win.

This time a bus was waiting for us outside the hotel. I was nervous but excited: during one of the endless breaks throughout that day's filming, the producer had explained to me that as charisma was one of the criteria in judging the winner of the *Lard* broadcast, each contestant would have a chance for a private, pre-dinner conversation with Max Terapia.

I'd never spoken with—nor do I believe that I'll again speak with—one of the chefs from the heroic period of Latin American cooking, so the ten or fifteen minutes allotted me seemed sufficient to avoid any unpleasant silences. I walked to the bus with the Venezuelan and the Argentine. The three of us agreed that the best thing about the trip was meeting Max Terapia. Once aboard the bus they split us up again.

I made the trip in silence. First, because of the rage I felt thanks to their treating us like children: each one of us had his own assigned seat. Next, because I was so nervous that I'd soon be meeting the legendary chef. Finally, because of how ominous the Suicide Building looked at night—we had to pass right by it to reach the city's nineteenth-century district. The turn round the traffic circle that ran below the building gave me the shivers once more.

The house where Max Terapia lives is nothing special: it's basically an old crumbling building on a commercial street. The ground floor has a rolling iron shutter and the only thing distinguishing it from the other buildings—this isn't obvious until you get close—is a security buzzer connected to a closed-circuit camera. My producer, the sole woman among eleven men, was also, amid a silence barely broken by sporadic whispers, the only one who dared press it.

Although I'd expected to be ushered in by some horror movie butler, it was Terapia himself who answered and then, a minute later, opened the door for us. He greeted us all, shaking our hands with a natural ease, the last thing I would've expected from a star of his caliber. He knew all six competitors by name. He pronounced mine with a Catholic schoolboy's accent appropriate to Lima's upper classes, noticeably weighting the first accented vowel then letting the rest fall into silence with princely disdain. Until that moment, I hadn't realized how my unease also came from the way people in Lima speak Castilian, working it between their tongue and palate with a jeweler's precision: like people from Mexico City, their delivery is grounded in verbal voluptuousness, not precise meaning. Terapia was dressed in some standard-issue drill pants and a sky-blue shirt. He looked older than the face on his cookbooks and memoirs.

The room we entered was dark, barely illuminated by the light from an enormous elevator, like one in a museum, standing open at the far end of the room. This is my younger son's sculpture studio, he explained as he led us toward the elevator. He lives in New York, Terapia continued, but he comes here to work in the winters because it's too harsh there. He pressed one of the buttons on the panel then turned to me. You live in Washington, don't you? Until that moment he had simply spoken by way of general announcement, the way famous people do so that everyone can enjoy their witty remarks. Yes, I told him, but the winters there aren't so cold. D.C. is in the South, two or three hours south of the Mason-Dixon Line. And do you return to Mexico often? The air thickened with a deadly electricity, produced by the others' jealousy at the prospect of my life seeming more interesting to Terapia than theirs. My producer was the only one who smiled when I said no, that I'd never returned since I left. The elevator stopped. I was like that when I was young, Terapia said, in London for nine years without returning to Peru, partly because I went into exile, and partly because I had no money. Then the door opened and we realized that the time we'd shared in the elevator was to be our moment of greatest intimacy with him: the flat where he lived with his wife had been converted into an enormous set for Swiss television.

They filmed us stepping out of the elevator, the introductions with Terapia's wife, our visit to the house's legendary nineteenth-century kitchen, our time in the living room chatting with the two of them, and the three or four minutes of theoretically private conversation enjoyed by each contestant. Of course they filmed the cocktails—I asked for scotch; my producer, to my surprise, wine—and the starters, ceviche again, this time with shellfish. The first course was fish soup, and the second, *pollo al ají*—chicken in spicy red pepper sauce. Next came salad to cleanse the palate, and for dessert, Venezuelan white chocolate cake and coffee. It was all very good and prepared with excellent taste, but also, following the style that made the master of the house a celebrity, with just a hint of *povera*: a constant, very lively flow of flavors with an accent on rawness and frugality.

At last we met the cook, a woman as old as the Andes from whom Terapia said he'd learned everything. I found

161

that last detail more than usually moving, in part because I too learned everything from the servants and the chauffeur, the ones truly responsible for the sentimental education of young Creoles in Mexico City. Also, the brandy I was drinking had by now helped me block out the cameras' incessant filming and all the lights surrounding us.

Shortly after ten o'clock in the evening the bell rang. Terapia told us not to worry, that it was some friends of his with whom he'd arranged to go out on the town; they thought that the dinner would be over earlier. If we wanted to, we could accompany them. I sensed my producer's alarm, and I whispered in her ear that we should take him up on this offer, it sounded like a good idea. She exchanged glances with her set manager and the other producers. The Argentine hastily said that it seemed like an excellent idea while the mulatto and I seconded him in the hope of getting the Swiss off our backs for once. The chief cameraman discussed it in a very low voice with two or three of his men then nodded his approval. My producer squeezed my leg under the table to show that she liked the idea, and I patted the back of her hand.

In all honesty, the night became much more enjoyable the moment we got back on the bus, everyone by now half-buzzed and the overall mood relaxed by the sweet hint of decadence that inevitably marks everything people from Lima do. Their feigned but ferocious humor, the grace with which they move about without seeming to touch the floor, their irresistible smiles, which in other circumstances would seem stiff and artificial, were very well-suited to a night together out on the town.

We went to a place quite nearby whose name I can't possibly remember. It was a gigantic club, some kind of industrial hanger, possibly an old marketplace, with hundreds of

162

tables crowded around a dance floor dominated by a band-stand. As one of the dolled-up women accompanying us explained—I was translating her words right into my producer's ear, my hand on her naked, sleeveless elbow—it was a club where immigrants from Puno got together to revisit old times, dancing to the rhythm of bands that played a new type of essentially eclectic pop music: turntables and panpipes, charangos and rhythm boxes, synthesizer waltzes. On the weekend—it was Friday—there was also a series of intermissions with performances of some rather homey folk dances whose authentic innocence, the woman said, made them worth seeing.

We sat at a gigantic table where they served us a complimentary Pisco Sour made from the strong Peruvian liquor of the same name, then filled the tablecloth with pint bottles of beer and some tiny glasses bearing the brewery name: *Cuzqueña*. By the time I realized it, I was dancing with the Swiss woman to the impenetrable Puno fusion. It seemed like my producer had never drunk more than a glass or two of wine. Now, thanks to the Pisco, she was noticeably relaxed. It was a sort of zero sum game: she'd never been treated as if her body was her most important asset, and I hadn't stepped onto a dance floor in years. While avoiding the mambo—I was really out of practice—I taught her to dance some rhythms related to salsa and cumbia. I could feel the moment she loosened up for me: when the lower back muscles—the ones you press to guide your dance partner—start trembling, you know that whether a woman is Calvinist, Catholic, or Jewish, you can get her into bed.

At this point it's probably already clear that in spite of my efforts to live like an exiled saint, I also know how to get into trouble. It's not easy these days to live like a monk, just as it wasn't in the seventeenth century; achievement matters less than determination. One more or one less *gringa* bouncing on my mattress springs in no way reduces the symbolic valor of my effort, and the archaic consistency of my cooking suffers more if I'm haplessly wasting the divine substance of my semen jerking off than if I occasionally sacrifice my vital precepts. In all my many days of weakness, whenever I end up bringing some customer home to my cell, I've never felt that I was being unfaithful either to my way of life or to my tormented memory of Teresa. If one of them occasionally—or frequently—woke up in my bed the next morning, it was because we went to sleep together drunk. I've never offered them breakfast and I've never slept with the same woman twice. Like priests, more than being celibate, I try to stay focused on the ministry to which I'm bound.

The Swiss woman and I had ended up at the opposite corner of the table from where Terapia was sitting. Nearly isolated, we were able to be more relaxed. During the set breaks, the folk dances, or the stretches of incomprehensible music, she chatted with the Paraguayan chef's producer—whom I began to privately suspect had been invited simply to round out the diversity of our group—while I talked with one of Terapia's friends. His name was Pablo and we were uncomfortably alike in height and complexion; the ten or fifteen years he had on me made him heavier, and his hair was quite gray, but we could have passed for brothers. He owned a very successful chain of coffee shops.

He seemed, for reasons that escaped me, somewhat deranged; he made unbelievably insolent remarks about the poor local folk-dancers, insulting them however possible whenever they passed near the table. Between one savage comment and another he maintained long, guarded silences, his eyes fixed on a woman—also middle-aged, very blonde and extraordinarily good-looking—who spent the whole evening hanging on Terapia's arm. Every once in a while he assumed an air of tremendous gravity, explaining to me with an anthropologist's precision the regional motifs one should look for in a dance. In those moments he showed himself to be far more fragile than his bastardly attitude revealed the rest of the time.

We got out of there around two o'clock in the morning, by which time I had the Swiss woman's heart in the palm of my hand, like a fresh-squeezed orange. I no longer remembered that the idea had been to spend the evening with Terapia when he said goodnight to us all in the aisle of the bus, followed out by a long line of his friends. The café owner was last. He had the arm of the middle-aged blonde woman, who barely said goodnight to us, attentive as she was to every gesture from the star chef up ahead.

Pablo told me he would call me early on Sunday, once the contest was finished, to show me around Lima: we'd ended up on friendly terms after I'd gotten totally fed up with his anthropological sentimentality: among the many dances that we saw, the one from Cuzco was the most peculiar because it had almost no traces of the Hispanic, African, and Chinese cultures which shaped modern Peruvian tradition. It was a leaping line of uproarious male dancers dressed in outfits with very wide sleeves. With each leap they made, they extended their arms and gave a harsh, ferocious, birdlike cry. With glassy eyes—whether from drunkenness or nostalgia for everything that we've all lost forever, I don't know—my confidant told me that it was a dance of the fallen Incas, of princes to whom nothing remained but the memory that they'd once been condors. Recalling how invincible Teresa made me feel when she believed that I was the historian Mexico needed, I thought I might collapse there and then. I felt obliged to explain the sadness that came upon me so visibly—Pablo put his arm around me—saying how the defeat of the Incas, the bottomless pit, reminded me of the Mexicans' own fall. Pablo told me not to worry, that people from Lima understood passion.

IV

I didn't go to bed with the Swiss woman that night because it wouldn't have been very ethical before the contest was finished—that's what she told me, anyway, though the idea had never crossed my mind. I didn't sleep with her the next night either because it would have been too depressing after my complete and utter defeat.

I was knocked out in the first round. I didn't even make it to the improvisations, which, given that I'm a methodical and insecure man, was where I thought I'd be disqualified. After the terrible moment when I found out that I'd been eliminated, the Argentine told me not to take it personally, that a Peruvian fellow like Terapia would never give the prize to a Mexican Creole like me. He said that both countries were too much alike, and that the Paraguayan was the one who was going to win: nobody had ever heard of his restaurant in Asunción, which would mean no new competition for Terapia. I don't know about the accuracy of every element of his theory, but regarding who would emerge as the winner, he was speaking with the voice of a prophet.

I didn't want to wait for them to finish filming, so I said that I was stepping outside the studio to smoke a cigarette, then kept walking to the street. I caught a taxi back to Miraflores where I drank three vodkas in a row at the hotel bar. After taking a nap I went out looking for bookshops to see if I could find some titles about convent life during Peru's viceregal era.

166

When I got back to the hotel, now late in the afternoon, I found a message from my producer—she was mostly angry because I hadn't been there to be filmed congratulating the winner, but still invited me out to dinner.

We went to a restaurant located at the foot of the magnificent ruins that Mr. Hinojosa had driven me past the night I arrived. We chatted like old friends: every defeat, I've noticed, brings us closer to our fellow sufferers, bound by that fatal, dispassionate knot that joins the survivors of great calamities. I didn't insist that she have a glass of wine. We talked a little bit about her job and a lot about mine; a little bit about her love life, absolutely nothing about mine.

We said good-bye in the hotel reception area: she was flying back to Geneva via New York on Sunday morning and I was leaving in the afternoon. I slept well in spite of, or thanks to, the fact that my room had a real bed, not the hard thin mat that I'd been stubbornly sleeping on since Teresa left me.

V

In the morning the phone woke me up. It was Pablo, Max Terapia's friend, who was inviting me to have breakfast at one of his coffee shops, after which he would take me to see the beaches so that I wouldn't leave without getting at least a glimpse of them. I told him that I preferred to visit the Gold Museum. He said that he'd observed the other night that I wasn't ready to see it, that it would be better if I visited it when I returned to Lima, wellcured of the sickness that was obviously tormenting me and which would not be helped by the sight of golden condors flying toward the sun all over the museum. Nobody had ever said anything so strange to me, so it sounded reasonable enough. I asked him to give me half an hour to get cleaned up.

We had breakfast in one of his cafés, on a street that reminded me intensely of the Colonia Roma in Mexico City. There, many years before, a restauranteur friend of mine named Raul had started promoting some of the recipes that I'd unearthed to write my book about Spanish colonial cuisine. It was Raul who found me in my apartment, almost dead of starvation, who knows how many weeks after that fucking whore Teresa had run off with my student. The very same Raul gave me a job at his place when we found out that they'd fired me from the university. At first, my job consisted of sitting in a chair behind the cash register, but, little by little, and mostly from pure boredom, I started working my way into the business and the kitchens. Less than a year later my friend introduced me to the gringo who wanted to open a restaurant serving nouveau-Mexican cuisine in the United States.

There was nothing spectacular about Pablo's coffee shop, although the food, like everywhere in Lima, was good. Among the numerous banalities we exchanged during breakfast, he asked me if the Swiss woman was beautiful. What, I said. I don't know, is she beautiful? How should I know, I answered him. Each to his own. So then you think she's beautiful. She's pretty, not lethal, I said, and he gave a start. What do you mean she's not lethal? he asked me. She's lived in Geneva her whole life, I told him, a city where you leave your bicycle parked on the street and nobody steals it. And if she moved to Lima? he asked me. I suppose after a while she'd learn how to style her hair, to steal her brother's bicycle—to be lethal. A look of horror crossed his face. Oh, you've got it bad, he told me. Really bad.

He took me around in his car to see a number of different places. We went to a couple of beaches and to a fantastic old bookstore owned by a Uruguayan—I walked out the door with a whole box of books. We ate lunch at a really expensive restaurant, even by Washington standards: built out on the water, surrounded by the ocean, and connected to the land by a long, narrow pier, it was called La Rosa Náutica. The idea was that you would feel like you were on a ship. Every so often he insisted on repeating his question, but by now he was answering himself: She was beautiful, wasn't she? Could she ever be lethal? I ignored him and asked if we could talk about politics or Peruvian history, which were the topics where his sharp, crafty wit shone best. We went to one of his other cafés for coffee and brandy—all his places had the same name but this one was really nice, located near the hotel so that we wouldn't waste time with the traffic and I wouldn't miss my plane.

The café was in a shopping mall with ethereal architecture: an extremely delicate structure that thrust out over the ravine. The café occupied the building's central location, so that one was seated literally above the abyss, from which the customers were protected by a railing and a rather tall partition of heavy glass.

I wore myself out praising the café's setting. Pablo told me that he was thinking of selling it, that having to clean the salt off the glass every day was too complicated. He waved his hands around too much while talking; I've been criticized for doing the same thing. The mall had been designed by a Catalan, he explained, who had not taken into account the locals' habit of leaping to their deaths. I had to install the glass myself to avoid negative publicity when someone ended up jumping off. And there's no built-in way for us to clean it; we've got to do it with scaffolding, every morning. It's super dangerous. I told him about my vertiginous fascination with Lima's penchant for flight. He made some rather nervous references to pre-Hispanic suicide practices, and mentioned aerial hara-kiri. He asked me if it was love-sickness that was tormenting me. Obviously, I said. It's the Swiss woman, isn't it? So she *is* beautiful, kind of lethal. It's not the Swiss woman, I told him. It's a long story, from a long time ago, and I really don't feel like telling it. Nobody, I concluded, can get so worked up over a Calvinist, believe me. You never know, he told me. My wife is Danish and I think she's sleeping with Terapia.

Glancing at his watch, he stood up abruptly, saying that he'd lost track of time, that he had tickets to take his kids to the soccer match, and would I please excuse him and catch a taxi back to the hotel. We shook hands with the tenderness of brother exiles. I stayed and ordered another brandy: I'd left my suitcases at hotel reception and I had a little extra time before Mr. Hinojosa would be coming by to pick me up.

I paid my bill, despite the waiter insisting that Pablo's friends didn't pay at his establishments. Walking out to the street I saw that on one of the shopping mall's balconies the management hadn't bothered to install any safety glass. A whole crowd of people was gathering there, looking down. Once inside the taxi I heard the ambulance sirens: another condor, the driver told me. On Saturday they finished work on the Suicide Bridge, so now they're coming over here.

LAST SUPPER IN SEDUCTION CITY

> . . . and the siege dissolved to peace, and the horsemen
> all rode down
> in sight of the waters

> St. John of the Cross

Friday, March 20.

As I saw the lights of Mexico City spread out below us before landing I caught myself mentally humming the tune of "Volver"—an unbearable affectation. Just as Carlos Gardel sings in that classic tango . . . *the snows of time have silvered my temples.* His turned silver because he was away for twenty years, mine because premature gray hair runs in my family: I'm condemned to suffer low-impact drama. I remembered my grandfather saying that Agustín Lara was a hick whose one single virtue was that he liberated us from the tango thanks to his impossible talent for composing boleros. Then I forced myself to think about Guadalupe Trigo, the later improviser of boleros, who says that at night the city dresses up like a mariachi. But that doesn't really describe it: it's more like the Milky Way, a sacred host of fire which you must swallow whole, without chewing.

I wonder what Teresa would think if she could see me with so much gray hair. Since I bought a computer for my apartment and managed to get myself online, I've been back in touch with *el Distrito Federal.* They tell me that she's been living in Mexico ever since she broke up with my student, that when she runs into one of our mutual acquaintances she always asks about me. I doubt that she's weathered the silent ravages of time very well either.

My mother and my sister picked me up at the airport. I will stay with them for the weekend and on Monday I'll go over to Raul's apartment: my family's house is too crowded—there I'll be better able to practice the monkish discipline to which I'm accustomed. They're not happy with the idea, but they realize that it's better than nothing. I'm going to stay with Raul through the week, then on Saturday and Sunday I'll be back with them again.

Monday, March 23.

Too much family. At my mother's house I was able to stick to my schedule, but the demand for socializing there is heavy: my brothers show up every little while with their wives and kids, and then my aunts and uncles come around, and then the visits with Grandpa who's been sick forever.

I'll be better here. I'm staying in a room that seems much more like my apartment in Mount Pleasant: a bed—iron, perfect for a convalescent like me—a table, and a wicker chair; it even has a window. The kitchen is an abandoned wreck—being a restaurant owner, Raul only uses it for making coffee—but I'll see what can be done. At any rate, I have enough business appointments the whole week to end up eating out every night.

Today we're going out to have a drink, for old times' sake. It's Monday, so I imagine we'll take it easy. I have a lot to get done in just a few days. Some gallery owners from Colonia Roma want to make me a business proposal. I don't feel quite ready to come back and live in Mexico City, but here I am, after all. Tomorrow I'm going to the Universidad Nacional to visit the archives at the History Institute. They've got a collection of women's letters from the colonial era that I've never heard about before. If I want to capitalize on my run of good luck that started after doing *Lard*, it's absolutely necessary for me to publish a cookbook: my tome about eating habits is too dense for the rather frivolous direction my life has taken, something I no longer really understand.

Tuesday, March 24.

I hadn't remembered Mexico City being so wild. We went to a simple, nicely designed bar where they serve tapas. Despite being Monday, it was full—it must have been past eleven o'clock when we got there. We were all chatting pretty carelessly. On a trip to the bathroom I ran into Esther, whom I'd dated back during the sad, hazy years of high school. She got married, then divorced, earned a relatively worthless postgraduate degree in France, and now she's doing well as a psychotherapist. She introduced me to her boyfriend. He's pretty much what you'd expect for someone in her situation: bald but otherwise hairy, almost fat, patient, well-intentioned. We didn't talk much. She's around 130 pounds, maybe 110, very curly blonde hair: a Polish princess maturing into a queen in exile.

When I returned from the men's room, Raul was already chatting with two women about a thousand years younger than us. Who knows where he found them. One was a big talker, over the top, perfect for him; the other one had crooked teeth but a moving smile. Esther walked by on her way out, and when she came over to say good-bye to me, told me it would be nice if we could chat, that we might see each other later at such-and-such a bar. It made sense to me because I was already drunk. Raul took notice.

We dumped the girls when it became obvious that they were too nice and modest—we left them in good company with a couple of lesbian filmmakers who might find a way to cure them—and we went to the bar where Esther was waiting for me.

She said Hi and I didn't peel my tongue off of hers until I got way down deep, far enough to taste the *café con leche* she'd drunk with her breakfast. I felt all the vertebrae in her tiny, childlike backbone, and she pretended to be indignant that I'd unfastened her bra in public. I told her I was so loaded she should be thankful I didn't just tear her shirt off. Now, up close to her, I admired once again her tiny ears with their little girl's shiny hoop earrings, barely visible. She smelled the same as always, the quasi-synthetic odor of distillation shared by all women who don't sweat. Before leaving we snorted some coke in the bathroom vestibule.

It was hard for us to walk because Esther was wearing a pair of jeans that were too tight to admit my hand, which I kept glued to her ass the whole time. I had to unsnap them before we could get comfortable in the back of Raul's car, where I went right back to groping the plush pissoir of her sex. Something inside of me made peace with my lost childhood—one without Baudelaire, without rhyme, without a sense of smell, as López Velarde said—as I kept on masturbating her in the back seat.

Once we got into the iron bed and carried out the first assault—pure muscle and fury for all our missed opportunities—she said, as she turned around and offered me her backside, that the second time she wanted me to put it up her ass. I started rubbing my nose up and down her milk-white spine, and then ran my tongue from the seam between her cheeks up to the back of her neck. We didn't do that when we were kids, I told her. She turned to look at me from the persecuted depths of her nearly transparent eyes, and said that her being married to the world's biggest idiot had at least been good for something. Then she began stroking my member with her hands. She meticulously examined my sex, running her fingertips along the folds of skin that were expanding from the miraculous touch of her skin and my memory. You're the only uncircumcised man I've gone to bed with, she told me. Then she asked me to stand up and she raised herself into a sitting position. She smelled it carefully, kissed it, and licked it from the scrotum to the bulb; she took it in her two hands and slipped the tip into her mouth. She caressed it slowly with her tongue, sucked on it, and tickled me at the base of my shaft. I turned her around again, working it between the hemispheres of her ass. She stretched out an arm from beneath her open rosebud and caressed my testicles. She turned and looked me in the eyes and said: Come inside, with her face somewhere between fear and fervor.

I slipped my penis in and out of her vagina several times to get lubricated. She was so worked up that my balls knocking against her clitoris stimulated her even more. She buried her face in the bed and opened herself up. I pushed inside and she gripped the edge of the mattress and yowled. Her back moved like one single muscle as it flexed with each new thrust. She took my left hand and clasped it to her breasts—overcome by gravity—snorting so wildly I thought it would earn me a standing ovation from the neighbors when I stepped outside the next day. We did it once more, this time with pure tenderness, before passing out.

I woke up really late, totally destroyed but still savoring a generous satisfaction. I rousted her out of bed and she told me not to worry, she had no patients until the afternoon. I told her I was in a hurry, that I had to go and do some research. I didn't even offer her an apple for the road. She asked me for the house phone number and I told her I didn't know what it was. Once I was good and sure that she wasn't going to return, I went back to bed.

175

Raul is taking a bath. I don't remember who he brought home, if he brought anyone, that is. We're going to go have lunch at a nearby restaurant—I'm in no shape to go to the market to buy any better ingredients than the horrors he's got in his fridge. The archives will have to wait until tomorrow; my pupils are shrunk down to pinpoints and the bright light from the copier would be unbearable.

Wednesday, March 25.

Tijuana. Around 130 pounds, maybe 110, gigantic eyes, matte-black hair, the occasional diabolic smile, married to something that seems like a Russian, slow but friendly. She used to go out with Raul until the days came when we all turned into predators of our own karma: they'd believed in the nice little house with flowers in the windows, in having little children, in taking them to Mass with their hair neatly combed on Sundays. When they broke up she took vengeance on him by sleeping with all his friends, which both did and did not include me: even though I'd always lusted after her, once I had her at my disposal, my loyalty to Raul proved stronger than my desire. Either that or I was really stoned and I just couldn't get it up.

We ran into her when she was having lunch with her husband at the restaurant, so we sat with them and started talking shit about half of Mexico City. We've got quite a few friends in common, Teresa among them—she told me that Teresa doesn't have anyone steady right now although she's got no lack of company, and insisted that she'd been asking about me. At a certain moment she discreetly placed her hand on my leg.

More people we know showed up: my first editor, the dyke filmmakers on whom we dumped those young girls last night—they still haven't forgiven us—another refugee from the history department who ended up a millionaire by founding his own crisis-management agency: specializing in World War II turned out to be good for something. He was with his wife and a baby. During dessert Tijuana sent her husband off to do some lowly errands, dispatching him with a wave like a goddess. Before he'd even finished saying good-bye she'd already moved her hand to my fly.

More people arrived along with the coffee: the culture editor for a magazine supplement and his assistant reviewer, a young man who must be his lover—even his wife calls him Socrates—and a movie critic I hadn't seen since graduate school, followed by his wife, who's obviously involved with Raul. We went to have some drinks at a place nearby. I stayed sitting at the bar chatting with Tijuana: she quit dancing, teaches Italian classes, eats lunch every day at her parents' house, and is generally happy. She had to get home at a reasonable hour and I wanted to get to bed early, so we left a little before five o'clock and went to a hotel that she suggested. They were offering a Tuesday discount and gave us a Jacuzzi suite for the price of a regular room.

The thing with Tijuana is that she always ended up causing a scene—there were so many times when we were younger that I pulled her out of some club totally bombed and half naked—so I just let her do her thing. You've got to treat me like your whore, she told me in an almost motherly tone as she sat me down on a tiny chair in the gigantic room they'd given us. Then she started undressing.

She's still got the same amazing body she had when she was young, except for her breasts, which have shrunk, thanks to the horrific diets I'm sure she follows. Her buttocks are full and high, her sex mysterious, nearly hidden beneath a thick, trimmed bush. She'd kissed me on the sly in the bar and then, in the taxi, with an almost painful intensity. Once we were in the room she didn't kiss me again until she was naked. She still smells like some stone-age fruit locked away in my Neanderthal memory, which is the one I access the most.

She removed my shoes and socks—the sole offensively placed on her thigh while she untied them—then stood me up and undid all my buttons. She showed a demonic smile when she felt my member lurking around, searching for the opening in my underpants. She played with it for a while, first with her hand and then with her nose and tongue. Once in bed, I first let my face melt into her vagina. Then I plunged in ruthlessly, ripping into her as she begged me through clenched teeth to grip her ass with both hands. Although she was soaking wet, she was still very tight, so we did a lot of wriggling and dancing, and as I started thrusting it felt like something ruptured: if our hips didn't synch up just right she dug her nails into the base of my spine. I asked her two or three times if I was hurting her; with glassy eyes she told me that was how she liked it.

We did it twice, almost back to back. In between I entertained myself playing with the fine soft hair that grows around her coccyx. I've got a little tail, she told me. We phoned her husband: she told him that she was out with Teresa and that they were heading to the movies. Then she phoned Teresa and told her that she was with her lover (another demonic smile as she rolled around on the bed), so would she please not call her house. We put on our underwear and sat down to chat in the little sitting room. We brewed some coffee and from her bag she produced a package of Choco-Rolls that made me melt with tenderness.

When I got up to piss she followed me. She watched the stream in a saintly rapture and stuck her hand into it. The liquid glazed her olive skin, ran down her fiery veins, splashing up in a tiny cascade as it struck her wedding ring and found its way blocked. When I finished, she caught the last drops on her index finger and brought them to the tip of her tongue. She licked her palm, then dried the back of it on her bush, which she went on playing with for a while. My turn, she said, and sat down on the toilet. Her glassy urethral pitter-patter started to wind me up again: I took off my T-shirt and pulled her nose to my belly button. She pulled down my boxers and took my member in one hand, my testicles in the other, smelling herself in the folds of skin. She licked and caressed it until it rose up. Wait for me, she said, tearing off a piece of toilet paper and standing to wipe herself. I grabbed her by the hand, pulled her to the bed and cleaned her off myself.

She rested her legs on my shoulders and I entered her from the front. Next, I turned her over and penetrated her from behind as she lay face down. I finished by taking her again from the front, her feet wrapped around my calves. We rose at least four inches in the air while I was coming.

Before heading back outside we decided to take advantage of the Jacuzzi. As I opened the faucets I suddenly felt like I had to go to the bathroom again. Don't waste your fluids, she told me, stretching out to lay back in the tub. The water barely covered her body. Piss on me, she ordered. After a moment of indecision I opened the floodgates and gilded her sex, her stomach, her breasts, her shoulders, her neck, her smile. She then pissed out her own waters into the tub. We made a pact: no soap or showering until the next day. And this? I asked her, pointing to the impossible erection that was starting to grow again. Masturbate, she said. Look right at me.

It was after ten o'clock by the time we finished getting dressed. She pulled out her cell phone, to call her husband I suppose. Before dialing she asked me where we were going to have dinner. I told her that she was eating at her house, I was having dinner with Raul like I'd already planned, and to call for two taxis.

I found him and the movie critic's wife in a rather mediocre French place where we'd agreed at midday to meet up. They were already finishing dinner when I arrived. By coincidence an old friend came walking by our table. He used to be a novelist and now works taking pictures of people's auras for curative purposes. I went off with him to a techno club so as not to inconvenience Raul and his lover at the house. We ended up dancing with some drop-dead ugly girls.

Thursday, March 26.

Susana. Bluish white, strong shapely legs, ethereal dress, expensive shoes, huge enigmatic purse. She went out for a while with Socrates when they both lived in London. She says that she's his best friend, and isn't sure if he does it with men, but that he definitely can't do it with women. Susana is my new editor's ex; his wife introduced her to me at breakfast when we were discussing the terms of the contract for my cookbook, on which I haven't made the slightest progress.

Susana has a research permit for the History Institute at the Universidad. The idea was that she'd take care of the paperwork so that I'd be able to study the letters before tomorrow, which will be my last working day in Mexico. She doesn't mess around: we were eating breakfast at a crêperie in San Ángel when she suddenly pulled a library catalog out of her bag. Without saying anything, she stood up and told me we were leaving because they were just opening up the archives desk at the university.

Once in the privacy of her Volkswagen she asked me

if I was the chef who ended up becoming famous because Teresa had dumped me. I told her that chefs weren't famous, and that those were two separate events; that I'd earned a certain amount of recognition because I have a disciplined imagination and a tremendous capacity for work, and that Teresa lost me because she was a stupid cunt. That made her laugh, and she told me that as soon as Teresa learned that I was going to sign with the publisher she started phoning her just as if they were best friends. She's looking for you, big guy. I shrugged my shoulders and said that she could find me if she wanted to. You'll see, she told me. Today she'll just casually show up when you're having dinner with those gallery owners from Colonia Roma. And how do you know who I'm having dinner with? I asked her. Now she was the one shrugging.

Of course it turned out to be impossible to gain access to study the damned letters. The best we could get was the vague promise that they'd scan them within a few weeks, and Susana would mail them to me. On the spot, she pulled the discs to burn them onto out of her bag. I asked her if she always carried around blank discs. She told me they were re-recordable, like her.

It was by now past twelve o'clock, so we went down to celebrate the snafu with a vermouth at a bar in Coyoacán with tables on its patio. We had lunch on the other side of the plaza, at a place with more sophistication than taste. Naturally she no longer felt like going back to the publishing house, so when we got around to her dropping me off at Raul's house, I invited her to come in and sleep it off, and then we could have a coffee. She thought that was a good idea.

She took off her dress and shoes in a flash and got right into bed under the blankets: houses in Mexico are always really fucking cold. Now lying comfortably by her side—chastely, I swear—I told her that she seemed to be the only thirty-something woman in Mexico that didn't have at least one, if not several, boyfriends. Not for long, was her reply: in my new role as a star of international gastronomy, I was going to need a real tough bitch by my side. Then she fell into a comatose sleep.

Her nose in my neck woke me up. She was lying comfortably on top of me, resolutely naked. You're really warm, she said to me when she noticed that I'd opened my eyes. I liked the smell of her fine, straight hair all mussed up, almost like a baby's. She flicked out the tip of her tongue and began licking up the sweat that had pooled in my collarbone, then she worked her way up to the embarrassing gob of saliva in the corner of my mouth. Before thrusting her tongue down to my tonsils she said that, yes, this was an ambush.

She yanked off the blankets and slid down to my knees. She pulled down my shorts as I took off my T-shirt, my calves clenched tightly between hers. She has a large mouth, just the right temperature; getting head from her was more like getting a massage than the kind of sharp pleasure that most women deliver. Give me something too, I told her, and she turned her body around so we formed a sixty-nine. To access her rather pale sex required parting the curtains of her fleshy lips. Quite suddenly, she raised herself into a squatting position, rearing and bucking, using my groin like a handhold.

She's got perfect breasts: round, high-set, intelligent. Grasping her thighs, I let her do the work but she didn't come until I stretched her upright, squeezing her breasts, her back arching sharply, her nails sunk into the backs of my knees. I laid her out beneath me. She clenched the bedstead rail, her breasts even more beautiful in repose. Like a salsa dancer, she had smooth, still shoulders and a voracious agitation in her legs and hips. Put your tongue here, she said, panting like a wounded doe, pointing her nose at her left armpit: I don't use deodorant. She'd spread herself out across the bed like a manta ray. I came for a long time, while she went on making even more noise. She wrapped her legs around mine and took advantage of my slow softening to masturbate by pressing her clitoris against the base of my pubis. I remember her spine pulsing from the successive waves of pleasure. She murmured: *my pleat, my pleat, my pleat*, from inside some joyous place where I was no longer present. After she stretched herself out again she spent a very long time running her fingertips up and down my shivering back. I fell asleep again.

She woke me when it was almost evening. You've got to get cleaned up, she said, so you can look handsome. I gave a little smile, trying to seem sweet. Don't look at me with that face like a toy clown: I'm sure it helps you to get laid, but it looks pretty lame to me. It's the only face I've got, I answered her. You're just sad because nobody's treated you like a star. She told me to turn over and then she gave me a massage from my neck down to the soles of my feet. When she finished I had an erection again. She hopped off the bed and said: Wait for me, just a minute. I planned on doing whatever she told me to. She reached for her bag and took out a silk scarf that she used to tie both my hands to the bed rails. She knelt over me with her open legs resting on mine, her whole sex exposed for my benefit, and began to masturbate with consummate skill. I'm dry, she said, speaking to herself, I believe, without the least affectation. She brought her sex close to me so that I could moisten it. At first my tongue burned from the lingering drops of my semen but soon enough I was going full steam again. She moved her hips in circles then suddenly said that was enough, pulling away from me and continuing to rub herself with her hand. At a certain point she gave a long sigh, went quiet, and then asked me to wait just a moment. She reached for her bag again and after digging through it a bit extracted a slender, elegant metallic vibrator. Do you always carry a vibrator in your purse? I asked with amused curiosity. "I'm only interested in really insecure guys, and, you know, they can't always . . . " she said. I thought about this later on and didn't find it so funny, but at that moment I wasn't in the mood for contemplation. She slipped the silver missile into her sex and turned the switch at its base, tensing and twisting as the vibration in her hand was transmitted throughout her body.

When she finished, her face wore a beatific smile. I was on the point of exploding. She grabbed hold of my sex and, waving the vibrator in the air, said to me: Your turn. Terrified, I had visions of a proctologist. Feeling my wrists tied tightly to the head of the bed I told her that I'd never done that and I wasn't at all interested. You're really stupid, she said, this one is vaginal; anal ones have a different shape. She grabbed her bag, slipped the metallic phallus back inside, then searched again through its interior. This time she took out a plastic bottle of honey. You carry honey in your purse? I asked her. It's for coffee, she said, I don't eat meat, so I've got to get my nutrients wherever I can. She popped open the top with her thumb, turned it over, and squeezed. A thread of gold spilled over my sex. Good little boys, she explained, come quickly when you do this to them because what happens is that the flavors mix. She closed the bottle, licking her finger. She put it back into her bag and fell to work voraciously. I came almost immediately. While she

184

was untying me she told me that the bastard's smile on my face had improved. Now, get cleaned up. You've got to look great, so that whore Teresa sees what she lost. Go on, you're already way ahead of the game.

By the time I got out of the shower she'd left. On the bed she'd laid out for me my best-cut suit with a French-collared shirt and one of Raul's Italian ties; he always spends more on clothes than I do. On the shirt was a note torn from a stenographer's notebook in which she'd written that she'd come by to get me at eight thirty, and that I shouldn't comb my hair until it was totally dry—that's the secret.

Dawn, Friday, March 27.

The gallery owners from Colonia Roma made me an offer: bring Los Empeños to Mexico City, its natural location. They showed me the house that a couple of them had just bought together; the restaurant would go on the ground floor. The location is unbeatable and they're prepared to invest in a kitchen that would be a faithful copy of the ancient ones I've envied.

Just as Susana predicted, Teresa appeared, now late, seated at the bar. She looked spectacular, more beautiful than ever behind the veil of an adult melancholy that I was not expecting. She was with someone. She's always been more skillful than me in the fine art of watching her ass. We exchanged kisses in the air—I liked the shape of her crow's feet—with the promise that we would talk; she introduced me to the millionaire she was with but I didn't even listen to his name.

When at last I was able to get away from the gallery owners I went down to the bar to look for her and they'd already left. The bartender handed me a napkin on which she'd written the name and address of a café near Raul's house,

185

saying that we should have breakfast at ten.

Not only am I going to go, I'd marry her again right this instant.

Monday, March 30.

I find airports and airplanes exasperating: we've only just taken off and I already feel exhausted. The worst is yet to come: passing through the police fortress the gringos have erected to protect their obese bodies from the muscular universe beyond.

I enjoyed spending Sunday at home with my mother and sister: I was able to rest a little, go to bed early, eat reasonably well, visit again with the endless parade of my brothers and their wives and their children—I had no idea whose they were; they all look like each other and like the rest of us. I found it very moving to see how eagerly they listened to the possibility that I might take up the gallery owners' offer and come back to Mexico. All this blood is your blood, said my sister after the second glass of anís, indicating the gathering around the table with a vague gesture that took in the whole family, as well as all those others who, at some time, had believed in the miracle of the Incarnation.

When I'd first arrived home, a little before midday, my mother was openly upset with me: Your aunts and uncles are pretty offended, she told me, that you haven't gone to eat dinner with them; God knows how many days Alicia spent making tamales for you. I told her that I'd already explained how I'd run into Teresa: I hadn't seen her in five years, we'd gone to lunch, and I was a total wreck when I called to cancel. It was better that way. You haven't seen your aunts, either, she said. But I was never married to any of them. That made her laugh. I shrugged my shoulders and told her to believe me, that it hadn't been easy. She nodded her head and pinched my biceps just like she did when I was little. It's all right, kiddo, stone has got to be stone.

During the meal everybody asked me—with ageless wisdom—how Teresa was doing, but without prying into any of the details of our meeting, which I suppose went very well. I arrived at the café a little bit after ten o'clock and she was already there, nervous; Mexican women, like their counterparts in Lima, are the last women on earth who maintain the mysterious art of knowing how to style their hair. Who knows if it's because they understand their body as one single harmonious mass, or because the bad taste of the hairdressers at large is so awful that they have to find some way to defend themselves. Contrary to all my own expectations, I acted like a wholesome, self-assured, grown man. She'd called in sick to work, so we had the whole day ahead of us.

We spent breakfast arguing, as if we were friends, the advantages and disadvantages of my moving back to Mexico, and some other minutiae: the eternal difficulty of her relationship with her parents, Tijuana's shortcomings, how fucked life in the United States really is—the word *Chicago* never passed her lips—her fantasy of being a professional hooker, and her inability to carry it off: I turned out more prude than slut, she told me. Up until that moment I'd had all my senses focused on the spiritual quality of her mature beauty: I'd arrived at the café with my fear of another rejection weighing much heavier than my desire to have her, but the image of her receiving a succession of unknown men gave me an electric jolt that was immediately translated into the memory of her body beneath mine and a rending of the veil way down deep in my testicles. I asked for the check. What are we going to do? she asked me. I told her we should stop by the market then go cook something at Raul's house.

She thought that was a good idea.

Leaving the café, it was no trouble at all to hold her hand while we walked along; I was telling her about the success my restaurant was enjoying thanks to the enormous public humiliation of being the first contestant eliminated from *Lard*. My clients began bringing their friends out of pure sympathy—it's true, I didn't say it just to amuse her.

I bought a big piece of rump roast so I could stuff it with pulped carrot and guava; also dried shrimp and rosemary for a broth; dragon fruit with cream and honey, amaranth, a chunk of heavy brown cane sugar, and pumpkin seeds to make *alegría* balls. We stopped to pick up a bottle of Ribera del Duero wine, and some Tehuacán spring water. Loaded down with shopping bags, we walked the four or five blocks that separated us from Raul's house, the sunlight streaming through the blossoming jacarandas.

While I unpacked the bags, she crouched down to check the oven—we had no idea if it worked. As she was walking by, taking the meat and the dragon fruit to the fridge, I calmly reached out and grabbed her ass as if we had never been apart. She stood straight up, turned around, and planted a tight, high-pressure kiss on my lips. We went running upstairs to the bedroom.

We undressed without any formalities. There was no strategic foreplay, simply the dialogue of tongues working as a metaphor for the communal vortex of the flesh and the desperate wish to disappear into its depths. To enter her body, to feel again the clean, precise embrace of her vagina— we're tailor-made for each other—was to return to a state of original, mysterious grace: achieving the shamanic power of entering the other, being transformed inside her, with her; becoming indistinguishable, like the spiraling, entwining strands of DNA in their mesmerizing chromosomal dance at the wondrous instant of conception.

I can scarcely recall the ghost of her tight lips, the color rising in her cheeks, her eyes so wide yet seeing nothing, because I no longer possessed a body. We synched up with the same steady rhythm as always. Our extremely slow ascent toward orgasm raised a heat wave that shook the curtains in the room. I clenched her hair in my teeth. Coming was like momentarily abolishing the opacities of the world and making it transparent, like a drop of saliva that contained the sketch of the universe that God never showed to anybody.

That's the paradox of what English speakers call *true love,* which I can find no way of correctly translating to Spanish, perhaps because in the end we always turn out to be bigger bastards. To be able to use the body to escape the body, to be transubstantiated into a mortal mess of secretions, to forget about oneself and the other, to be nothing but a surface: the odor we give off, the oils that lubricate us, the skin that protects us. To be a nameless sum of muscles and fat. To feel pleasure is to trade the body for bodily sensation; sex at its best is the most spiritual experience available to us.

I returned to wandering her back, the ridge of her coccyx, her buttocks. I let my fingers play in the tiny bushland around her ass and masturbated her to a climax, and then I entered her from behind, my hands squeezing her fists.

The third time she sucked me. With Teresa I take more pleasure in giving than in receiving, so that when I felt myself on the verge of exploding I told her I wasn't going to hold out much longer, and how did she want us to do it? She rose up and without unclenching my member she told me that she wanted me to come in her mouth, that I could take however long I wanted but I should drown her in semen. I sat up comfortably against the headboard to get a better view. She curled up perpendicular to my body

189

and scooted forward a little, so that I could put my hand between her thighs or her breasts, follow the curve of her back down to her buttocks, and play with her toes. When she felt like that was enough, she opened my legs and dove between them. She looked me in the eyes and said: Come. I did so, exorbitantly, until it hurt. She gave me a salty kiss and thanked me. I lost myself in an almost dreamlike trance and slipped into sleep.

I was awakened by her riotous laughter—like shrieking in a cathedral—mixed with the deep sound of Raul's voice. I got out of bed, put on my shorts to go to the bathroom and, in that near state of grace, descended to the kitchen. It turned out that besides Raul and Teresa, who were drinking some tequila in the living room, in the kitchen there were also—knocking back their first drink and gossiping in whispers, surely about me—the movie critic and his wife, Socrates and his young lover, and Tijuana sans husband. Teresa gave me a long kiss and sent me to say hello to the other guests, among whom I went delivering hugs and kisses. Tijuana stuck a finger in my belly button and told me I looked very cute. I told her that I'm no angel.

We chatted about nonsense while I brewed myself a cup of mint tea. When it was ready, Socrates poured in a little tequila and told me that they'd heard I was going to do the cooking; that was why they all came over. I told him that I'd need some galley slaves because people were already hungry. Tijuana and the movie critic volunteered to help, and the others went to the living room. Teresa came in with a stack of pots and pans.

I set Tijuana to prepare the brown sugar and Teresa to cut the dragon fruit. I gave the movie critic—clearly the least talented—very specific instructions for how to prepare the shrimp broth, handing him the little bunch of rosemary that he had to use, and precisely measuring the salt and the water, never taking my eyes off him. I sliced open the roast, so fresh that it was dripping blood. I set my cutting board next to the one Teresa was working on. Her hands were stained with the vegetable blood of the fruits—she was slicing them with careful devotion, as cleanly as coins. Another tequila. We made potatoes with the remaining rosemary and a jar of mole sauce we found in the refrigerator. When the critic finished with the broth—anyone else would have done a better job in half the time—I set him to work peeling carrots. We heated the oven and I suddenly remembered the hellish family dinner awaiting me at home. I called my mother to cancel.

When I came downstairs again, Tijuana and Teresa were waiting for me in front of the bag of guavas without the least idea what to do with them. It's an Aztec game: you've got to split the fruit in half and remove the pulp that surrounds the seed as if it were a heart, then you've got to peel it with the same tender loving care as if you were bathing a little child. We didn't have a fourth knife sharp enough for the critic to use, nor enough faith in his ability to carry out such a delicate operation: what remains of a guava after the sacrifice is an extremely delicate little rosy pink strip barely an eighth of an inch thick, just a leftover, which is, simultaneously, the sweetest and most sour thing in the world, and which denotes the metaphysical nature of Baroque cuisine: more theory than food. I told them that rump roast stuffed with guava pulp was the favorite dish of Bishop Palafox. It's out of this world, I said, the meat enveloping the remains of something that no longer has either an inside or an outside, just like the sacred host.

And my vagina, said Tijuana, sticking a finger in her mouth. She pulled it out shining with saliva and slipped it into Teresa's mouth. We made the guava paste in the same bowl in which we'd cooked the sweet base for the *alegría* balls. I stuffed the roast while Teresa poured the cream over the dragon fruit and Tijuana mixed up the pumpkin seeds and amaranth with the honey and brown sugar.

By the time I finally put the meat in the oven I was exhausted. Teresa gave Tijuana a long kiss and she slipped her hand into my shorts. I let her do it for a moment, but at last I decided it's always better not to mix things up too much, so I went upstairs to get dressed. They stayed a while longer in the kitchen. When I came in for a glass of wine to take with me to sit down in the living room they were chatting.

Everything turned out really well: we talked, we ate, we drank like gluttonous patricians. We sat over our coffee and brandy until very late, rendered every moment more civilized by the work that our excesses perform on the soft, pulpy flesh of our sad human lives.

Teresa helped me to clean up afterward and then spent the night. In the morning I didn't even offer her a cup of coffee.

Mexico City—Washington, D.C.—Mexico City,
1996–2004

ÁLVARO ENRIGUE was born in Mexico in 1969. He is an essayist, critic, professor, and the author of several novels and short story collections. His first novel *La muerte de un instalador* won the 1996 Joaquín Mortiz Prize. In 2007, the "Bogotá39" project named him one of the most promising Latin American writers of his generation.

BRENDAN RILEY has worked for years as a teacher, translator, writer, and editor. Among other works, he is the translator of Carlos Fuentes's *The Great Latin American Novel* and Juan Filloy's *Caterva*, both for Dalkey Archive Press.

FOR A FULL LIST OF PUBLICATIONS, VISIT:
www.dalkeyarchive.com

SELECTED DALKEY ARCHIVE TITLES

FOR A FULL LIST OF PUBLICATIONS, VISIT:
www.dalkeyarchive.com